TEA *and* CRUMPET
A British LGBTQ Anthology

TEA *and* CRUMPET

A British LGBTQ Anthology

EDITED BY UK MEET ACQUISITIONS TEAM

jms books

TEA AND CRUMPET

JMS Books LLC
10286 Staples Mill Road # 221
Glen Allen, VA 23060
www.jms-books.com

ISBN: 978-1-61152-146-7

Printed in the United States of America

CONTENTS

Introduction

WHAT DO YOU get when you invite a group of romance, gay lit, and erotica authors to embrace their British voice and examine what it means to be queer in Britain?

The answer is this anthology, a collection of positive LGBTQ stories with a decidedly British flavour. Take a journey with us through the British Isles: from the rugged coast of Ireland, via our sprawling cities and bustling towns, through to the sheltered seclusion of our English churchyards. Meet adventurous Scotsmen, Irish fishermen, and English characters from across the class spectrum. Step back in history to Elizabethan England and the early twentieth century, or slip sideways into a rural fantasy land.

All of these stories deal with same-sex relationships, although they are not all romances in the usual sense of the word. While we have plenty of stories of relationships just starting, there are also stories that deal with reconciliation after a break up, such as "We'll Always Have Brighton" and "Bloody Mathematicians". We even have a tragedy in the form of "Silent Witness", and a couple of stories with more ambivalent endings where the main character cannot see a way to the love they crave: "Fantasy Man" and "Frozen Angel". "The Utterly True History of Guy Alien and the Rise and Fall of His Band X Wing" gives another take on relationships, where a failed one is examined from a point in the future when the narrator has found happiness.

However, the majority of the stories are romances of a kind, from those that tease us with just a glimpse of first interest, to those that are unabashedly erotic. The one thing they all have in common, though, is their connection to British life with its tensions between tradition and the pull of the new. Read romances between conservative and punky women in "What Katy Did on Holiday" and "Beside the Seaside", and between men of different classes in "Fighting Cocks" and "Good Breeding". Meet gay couples who cross borders of race in "Blooming Marvellous" or nationality in "A Naughty Trip". Find out how a clergyman follows his nature in "Sweet Temptation", and discover just how sexy cricket whites can be in "On the Pull". See how love blossoms among the morris dancers in "Riding With Hob", under canvas in "Making Camp", behind the scenes at a royal wedding party in "Jeu d'Esprit", and down the local pub in "Matter of Opinion".

While the stories make use of icons of British culture, the writers refuse to resort to cliché, giving us a fresh and vibrant take on queer life in Britain, past and present. What's more, they are written with authentic slang and dialect, too often ironed out by non-British publishers. Have a bloody brilliant time getting down and dirty with the Brits!

I would like to thank all the authors for their generosity in providing their stories for free, so that the profits from this anthology can be used to help fund an annual convention of GLBT fiction in the UK. If you enjoyed their contributions, please show your gratitude by going out and buying some of their other work. I would also like to thank Alex Beecroft, Charlie Cochrane, Clare London, and JL Merrow for volunteering to help me select and edit the stories, and to Serena Yates for proofreading. Without you all, this anthology would never have been possible. Cheers, me old muckers!

Josephine Myles, June 2011

Making Camp
by Clare London

YOU SEE, I don't do *canvas*. You know…the camping thing.

I never have done. I'm a London lad: I thrive on the aggressive noise of the city and the frantic haste of its people. I like to smell the dirt steaming off the pavements on a wet autumn day, to pass graffiti-decorated brickwork and peeling pub signs on my way home, to hear the hiss of buses and inhale their diesel-breath. What's not to love in all that invigorating, infuriating, intoxicating glory?

Then came that Thursday morning.

"This is your chance," said my friend, Em. She leaned over my desk, peering at me. Her whole demeanour wasn't so much giving me friendly advice as threatening me with dire consequences if I didn't obey. "Christ, Nick, you've been going on to me about Max for months. This is your chance to go out with him this weekend, to talk to him about something other than the feature on defragging in PC Geeks Monthly, or whatever it is he has rolled up in his back pocket. I'm sure he *likes* you. You know. That way." She leaned in even farther, now winking lecherously, rattling my pencils and my equilibrium in equal measure.

I glared back. "You do know where he's going?"

She shrugged. "Somewhere in the West Country. Sun and

scenery, just a short break." She cleared her throat. "Not that I eavesdrop or anything."

"I mean *exactly* where." I frowned. "It's to a campsite. He's camping. In a tent."

She rolled her eyes. "And he wants you to go with him. I heard him say so." She smirked with indecent triumph. "He stood right here in front of your desk, turned his back on all of the girls in Cash Processing, and he invited *you*."

I blushed. I hadn't done much of that since the new clerk in Underwriting touched me up at the Christmas party then protested he'd been looking in my pocket for a pencil sharpener. I'd been wary of mixing business with pleasure ever since and, some would say, understandably. "I can't go." Time for *my* eyes to roll. "It's outdoors!"

"Nick, don't be a jerk," she snapped, and glanced over her shoulder. Max was in the next door office, right now, as I well knew. Stalking his online diary was a guilty secret of mine that I shared with Em alone. Unfortunately, that fuelled her matchmaking, which currently consisted of pulling the plug out of my hard drive and calling I.T. Support, several times a week. Humiliating, but it had the desired effect, bringing Max to the rescue every time.

And I never complained.

In fact, I was a lost cause, lovesick from the day Max joined the company. All three departments on the first floor went to the pub after work to welcome him, where he told us he'd been transferred from a remote branch office that clung to the cliffs of the West Country coastline, where (he claimed) the strong wind could blow seagulls off course, and you only got a decent mobile signal on alternate Tuesdays. We all laughed, and so did he. He told a very good story. I made some Town/Country Mouse jokes and he joked back, warning me the green fields would probably make me hyperventilate. But I remember I gazed at his friendly grin, his natural tan and his bright eyes, and I knew I wanted more of him.

"Say yes," Em hissed, her hands all over my keyboard. I tried to push her away but she was a woman on a mission. In just a few disruptive moments she'd creased up half the papers on my desk and moved everything out of place. "Say *yes*."

"No," I said, firmly. I snatched up my Routemaster novelty mug like a talisman. "And what happened to my coffee?"

"I've poured it over your keyboard and Max is on his way round."

"You've w*hat*?"

"Say yes to this weekend, Nick, or I swear, the graffiti about you in the Ladies' won't stop at the pencil sharpener incident."

Graffiti? *The pencil sharpener incident?* "Who told you about...?"

But Em had darted back to her own desk with another wink, and Max was threading his way across the department towards me with that deliciously cheerful, downright healthy grin of his. He had a bold, sauntering walk and broad shoulders, with a head of curly hair that started each morning with a sensible parting, but invariably lost the battle by lunch. Add to that the sky-blue eyes, and fresh, freckled skin that crinkled at the corners of his generous mouth when he smiled, and it was a very tempting package.

If that's what a country life does for you, I thought, it can't be all bad.

And so, when he asked again about us going away Friday after work, I said yes.

▲

SATURDAY MORNING, I awoke to a trumpet call from Hades itself, or that's how it sounded: a wailing scream, a shriek of hate and despair, ripping through the dawn.

Heart pounding with shock, I scrabbled out of my (borrowed) sleeping bag, cursing whoever had twisted the zip up between my arse cheeks while I slept. The traffic had been so bad the previous evening, we'd arrived really late at the campsite, and there'd been no time for anything except putting up the tents and crashing out. This morning, I barely remembered where I was, let alone why I wasn't waking to decent rock music on my digital radio alarm. I blundered into the side of the (also borrowed) tent, breathing harshly, wondering if oxygen were available for those with an allergy to polyester. My elbow thumped the tent pole at the doorway and the whole structure shuddered around me.

When I lurched outside, the fresh air hit me like chemical warfare, my bare toes curling up with the shock of grass underneath them so early in the morning. There was a sudden flurry of black feathers as birds launched themselves from the nearby trees. I stared at the world through dilated pupils, panting, expecting to see the Four Horsemen charging in on some satanic version of a tractor.

Instead, only Max was there, crouched outside his own tent, his back to me. He was dressed in just his shorts and he looked completely at home, stirring away at something in a pan, its surface bubbling and the sharp tang of its sauce catching in the back of my throat. I peered over at the pan, suspiciously. Was he going to eat that? From what I could see, it looked like it'd been vomited up by the Beast of Exmoor.

As I groaned and grasped the tent pole for extra support, his head whipped around. "What is it?" He looked concerned. "The crows wake you up?"

I never got time to reply with something witty and face-saving because we were both distracted by a strange creaking sound. Max stood up, abruptly, still clutching the spoon, globules of sauce dripping from its end. His eyes widened. The only other warning I got was the flapping sound of a loosened flysheet, and then the heavy rustle of canvas crumpling down on itself.

I stood there, staring resolutely and helplessly forward, listening to the dull twang of the poles springing free behind me, bouncing against each other, scraping down the seams of the tent. Then the muffled clang of them hitting the ground.

I thought I'd knocked each peg securely into the field the night before, but…maybe I hadn't.

There was a final thump and everything went quiet again. I didn't dare turn around. I coughed from a light mist of grass seed in my throat. A stray acorn rolled past my foot. Max's gaze shifted from over my shoulder and down to a point barely six inches from the ground.

"Shit," he said, thoughtfully. "Looks like the guy-ropes weren't tightened properly."

"I know nothing about tents," I said, defensively, but I knew the music had to be faced. Turning slowly, I surveyed the damage, my face hot with embarrassment. The whole structure was a tumbled mess on the ground, like someone had pulled the plug on it and let it fall where it liked. One of the metal posts had ripped a jagged hole through the fabric and was the only thing still propped upright, saluting the sky like a raised fist, claiming revenge against all camping virgins. To me, it was nothing more than a smashed jigsaw puzzle and I had no idea what piece went where.

Max started laughing. I sighed and turned back to face him, but now his gaze was fixed on my waist region.

"You buy those in town?" he asked, grinning. "You don't get that sort of thing down here, you see."

I didn't dare look down at myself. I felt that sick lurch in the gut that you get when you know your life is about to end, and in great and glorious humiliation. My hand hovered protectively in front of my groin, but the damage was done. I was standing in the middle of a field in broad—if early—daylight, with the rude reminder I was dressed in nothing but the Pokemon boxers that Em had bought me last year.

"I couldn't look more of an arse, could I?" I said, hoarsely. I knew what graffiti joy this would bring Em, if she ever heard about it. "Can I start the day again?"

Max shook his head, slowly. "Don't see how. But who cares?" He was still smiling, and his eyes were brighter than before.

Was that only because of the absence of carbon monoxide fumes down here? "Come and eat, we'll sort your tent out later." He reached out a hand and touched my bare shoulder, as if consoling me. "You can share mine tonight, no problem."

"I can change—"

"You look pretty good to me," he interrupted. His cheeks were flushed. I'd assumed that was from the cooking.

I sat beside him on the blanket and helped serve up the breakfast. Not beast's bile, but sausages and spicy beans, combined in a handy can, or so the label said. It smelled a hell of a sight better than it looked. Tasted good, too. After a while, it didn't feel so bad, sitting around outside in my underwear. Max was dressed just as sparingly, and he looked great. His chest was tanned like his face and arms, and he was just muscular enough for my liking. We looked at each other, looking at each other: then we smiled at ourselves and relaxed.

The sun was still pale, and the air was crisp, but neither of us seemed to feel the cold. He kept serving me more food, his hand brushing against mine. The sliced bread tasted like fresh-baked, the coffee had a rich hit I never got in my daily, franchised cappuccino. I laughed about my disaster and he laughed about some of his own. Time passed, comfortably enough.

He said I looked pretty good. My mind kept returning to that, and my stomach knotted with excitement.

And he said I could share his tent. Didn't he?

Maybe I didn't want to start this day again, after all.

▲

FRESH AIR IS really tiring, you know? I never realised how much. A stroll over the hills, a pub lunch and a game of one-on-one football, and I was in bed by nine. That is, in Max's bed. Well, sleeping bag, actually. They have that design nowadays, you know, where you can zip two of them together and make a double. It's very efficient.

Listen to me, the field and trek salesman. I'd never imagined this day ending up the way it did. Or let's say, I hadn't dared to hope.

At the end of the astonishingly tiring day, we had an al fresco supper of cold meat, bread and fruit at the camping site. We sat comfortably on the blanket at the tent's opening, munching slowly, drinking a couple of beers, chatting about what we'd seen and where we'd been. Nothing serious, nothing tense. But we were watching each other all the time, just like at breakfast, and just as coyly. Max said he hoped I was having a good time and I nodded back. He might have been asking me to prostrate myself on a local burial mound dressed in cow shit and brambles for all I cared. By then, I just liked nodding to him. His cheeks were shiny after the day's outdoor activity and his conversation much more relaxed than the technical troubleshooting sessions at work. And he hadn't teased me about the collapsed tent more than half a dozen times. I was in seriously besotted mood.

And he liked me too, I was pretty sure of it. He kept grinning at me, shifting nearer each time he reached for more food or drink. The light dimmed over the fields slowly and sweetly, the day's sun seeping into the horizon with a rosy glow. The air smelled of cut grass and hedgerow flowers. I stopped wondering how I'd fill the evening without the telly, and when my mobile phone bleeped a warning it was running out of battery, I pushed it away into my bag. My heart beat seemed slower, my breathing deeper. Or maybe that was because of Max.

It seemed we were both nervous that way, when in all honesty you both want to do it, and you both *know* you do, but neither wants to look like they're desperate or predatory. Max made some joke as to when I was going to start hyperventilating, and I laughed and said I reckoned the Town Mouse had given the Country Mouse a good run for his money on the football field. After all, he'd never have scored that second goal if I hadn't been distracted by a pheasant darting out of the trees and across the grass like it was late for the last bus. When Max didn't knock that witticism back to me, I paused and stared. His eyes suddenly darkened, then he curled a hand behind my neck and pulled me against him for a kiss. A long, wet and greedy kiss. And another.

Supper was rushed, after that. Desperate and predatory wasn't the half of it. And soon we were cuddled up inside a sleeping bag that was plenty big enough for two slim young men to stretch out, except those young men actually wanted to get up close and personal.

I had to admit, the noises were still odd, or the absence of them. None of the normal city traffic or sounds of a twenty-four-seven life. Just the crows calling the night in, the occasional sheep bleating in a distant field, the scurry of unfamiliar night animals under the trees.

However, inside the combined sleeping bag, it was far from hardship. If I really wanted, I could imagine I was at home with the central heating humming in the background and the Chinese takeaway three doors away. But after a while, when Max's mouth slid away from mine and he started licking his way down my chest towards my belly, I wasn't interested in imagination at all. He was strong, the muscles living up to their promise as he gripped my hips. Dirty talk was exciting in his soft West Country burr. His grin—the delicious one—felt even better when his mouth was wrapped devotedly around my dick.

"I'm not usually that loud, you know," I murmured. An hour or so after the exciting scrabble for nakedness, exploration and orgasm, we were clasped together warmly in the sleeping bag, both of us having come very satisfactorily and very enthusiastically. Twice. The taste of his sweat was still on my tongue, salty and tantalising. "Good thing there's no-one else camping in this field."

He sniggered and yawned, and I was secretly proud of having worn him out. "Yes, damned good," he agreed, sleepily. "But I made sure of it. I know the farmer who rents it out."

Made sure of it?

"And I'm sort of glad my tent collapsed," I said. "It got me in here with you." I laughed, rather awkwardly. "I still feel stupid about that."

"No need," he whispered in my ear. "I made sure of that, too."

"Are you saying it was your fault, my tent falling down?" His hand crawled around my waist and his lips were damp against my cheek, which was pretty distracting, and in all the right ways. But he was confessing to setting me up, wasn't he? What a bloody nerve! "What the hell did you do?"

"Just accelerated things," he said, softly. "Just got tired of fixing your hard drive and never getting more than a smile."

I swallowed hard. "You've been interested all this time?"

He made a huffing sound. *You took your time*, it implied.

I was suddenly nervous. "You didn't read any...graffiti about me, did you?"

He laughed, dismissing my nonsense. "No." His cock was hardening against my thigh. Maybe he wasn't as worn out as I'd thought, but didn't I say, I'm not the complaining kind?

"Your friend Em said you didn't do the camping thing." He shifted carefully, nudging his knee between my thighs. "But is this so bad?"

His skin was warm and sweaty against mine and I tightened my grip in his hair. "No," I murmured back. "Not so bad at all."

The distraction certainly worked for me. I rolled over in the sleeping bag, gasping and laughing and holding him tightly. Maybe this time around *I'd* be the first one to get worn out. Camping suddenly seemed the most attractive thing on my agenda. Maybe I'd even look into getting my own tent. Or just a bigger one for the pair of us?

Max hissed at me to pay attention to the matter in hand, his breath hot on my arse, his teeth nipping playfully at the crease of skin between buttock and thigh.

It was an invigorating, infuriating, intoxicating glory of a very different sort.

About Clare London

CLARE LONDON TOOK her pen name from the city where she lives, loves, and writes. A lone, brave female in a frenetic, testosterone-fuelled family home, she juggles her writing with the weekly wash, waiting for the far distant day when she can afford to give up her day job as an accountant. She's written in many genres and across many settings, with novels and short stories published both online and in print. She says she likes variety in her writing while friends say she's just fickle, but as long as both theories spawn good fiction, she's happy. Most of her work features male/male romance and drama with a healthy serving of physical passion, as she enjoys both reading and writing about strong, sympathetic and sexy characters.

Clare currently has several novels sulking at that tricky chapter 3 stage and plenty of other projects in mind...she just has to find out where she left them in that frenetic, testosterone-fuelled family home.

All the details and free fiction are available at her website. Visit her today and say hello!

Website: clarelondon.co.uk
Blog: clarelondon.livejournal.com
Facebook: facebook.com/clarelondon
MySpace: myspace.com/clarelondon
Twitter: @clare_london
Goodreads: goodreads.com/clarelondon
GLBT Wiki: bookworld.editme.com/clarelondonbooks

don't you, Wayne, love?"

"Er..."

"I met him on Mykonos. Went on one of them Club 18-30 holidays with your Auntie Sharon—you'll love her, Wayne, she's a right laugh. He used to work at this bar on the beach. Dead handsome, he was—you look just like him, love. He used to give me free drinks, he did."

Shardonnée cackled in an uncanny imitation of her mother. "Wanted to get his end away, din't he? God, Mum, didn't you know *anything* when you was my age?"

"And his name?" Giles asked hurriedly.

"Now, what the bleedin' 'ell was it? Stavros? It'll come to me, I know it will." Angie pursed her lips. Her lipstick bled up into her wrinkles in a fine illustration of capillary action. "Well, it wasn't Davros, I know that. Sorry, love, it was a long time ago."

"And she was pissed off her head," Shardonnée muttered.

"I got some pictures, though," Angie said brightly. "Where'd I put them pictures, Shards?"

Shardonnée sneered and shrugged, her top falling off one shoulder to display a greying bra strap. Angie tottered on high-heeled fluffy diamante slippers to a stack of magazines. Sifting through several trees-worth of *Take a Break* and *The Sun* (the latter all folded to page three, so Giles was treated to a rapid succession of naked breasts of varying size from "obviously fake" to "frankly ridiculous") she eventually unearthed a photo album bound in cracked PVC. Sitting next to Giles on the sofa, she opened it up.

"Here we are. That's me..." She pointed to a rather pretty-looking girl in a bikini. "And that, love, is your old man." With a sinking feeling, Giles stared at proof positive that this wasn't all some nightmarish mistake. The young man in the picture looked *exactly* like him. Same curly dark hair, same broad shoulders, same hirsute chest that had been a source of acute embarrassment since Giles was fourteen. "I do love a man with a decent chest on him." Angie grinned, and dug Giles in the ribs with that razor-sharp elbow of hers. "And see? I wasn't bad looking in my day, neither."

"I think you've hardly changed a bit," Giles said gallantly.

"Get on with you! Ooh, you're a one!" Angie squealed, while Shards made throwing-up noises, and Pete grunted "Hrrn, hrrn," which Giles took to be his version of laughter.

"Now, you tell me all about them posh lot what adopted you."

Giles sighed, and started to tell her about Mummy and Daddy. This was going to be a long visit.

▲

MUCH, MUCH LATER, having only escaped by promising to come back soon, Giles sat on the steps of his parents'—his *adoptive* parents'—conservatory. He had a large glass of single malt whisky in his hand and was staring into the pitch dark garden beyond.

Oz sat next to him, chugging down his third bottle of Insanely Bad Elf. He'd been a bit quiet since Giles had got back.

"I always wondered, you know?" Giles said, gesticulating with the Edinburgh crystal in the vague direction of the water feature. "What sort of people my parents were. Were they romantic, idealistic? Or hard-working, salt-of-the-earth types? And now I know." He paused dramatically. "I'm the son of a chav. A stiletto-wearing, chardonnay-swilling, chain-smoking, perma-tanned chav. And a Greek waiter whose name she can't quite recall." He hung his head in despair.

Oz nodded, patting him on the shoulder sympathetically, if a bit unsteadily. "Cheer up. It could have been worse."

Giles looked up, incredulous. "How? Just *how*, precisely?"

Oz glared at him. "Well, she could have been a raging snob like her son, for starters! Bloody hell, Giles, have you listened to yourself? This is your mother you're talking about! Have some respect!"

"What, I'm supposed to respect her for being careless

about contraception?" Giles's sneer turned abruptly into a grimace of pain. "Ow! That hurt!"

"It was bloody well meant to. That poor woman spent nine months carrying you in her womb, then endured hours of agony just so she could push your ungrateful self out into the world! If she could hear you now, I bet she'd wish she'd never bothered—just gone the easy route and flushed you down the toilet at six weeks gone!"

Giles shuddered. "You don't mean that, do you?"

Oz waved his glass, and Giles ducked to avoid a nasty contusion. "Well, yes. There she was, still in her teens, pregnant and alone. I bet nine girls out of ten would have been down the abortion clinic straight away. And for God's sake, she welcomed you into her home! Killed the fatted calf, so to speak—"

"That'd be Darren," Giles muttered.

"—and gave you a mother's blessing. A lot of women would have just slammed the door on you;"

"You never mentioned she might do that this morning!"

"—would've been embarrassed to see you standing there on the door step. A reminder of past mistakes and all that."

"All right, all right. Point taken." Giles looked gloomily at a moth that had landed in his whisky. It flapped pathetically a few times in the amber liquid then seemed to give up the fight. He fished it out and tried to blow on it gently with the vague idea of drying it out, but a slight misjudgement resulted in it flying from his fingers and disappearing in the darkness. Not, unfortunately, of its own volition.

Giles raised his glass and drank a solemn toast to its passing. Then he gagged, realising he was drinking something the horrid little insect had very likely peed in.

▲

AFTER OZ HAD stomped off to the guest room, Giles spent a restless night. Was he really being classist? Ungrateful?

He thought of Angie, and the way she'd smiled at the sight of him. Had there been a suspicion of a tear in her over-made-up eye?

"Mummy," Giles said next morning, hovering by the Aga as his mother did something complicated with the pressure cooker, "am I a snob?" He'd made sure Oz was safely occupied with the PS3 and out of earshot.

His mother turned, a picture of elegance as always. He'd spent many happy hours, as a child, trying on her wardrobe of frothy chiffon dresses and crisp linen jackets. And the shoes…High ones, and low ones. Shoes of every style and hue, some of them custom-dyed to match particular outfits. Delicate strappy sandals, and cheeky little peep-toed courts…Really, it was quite astonishing that it'd taken him until he was seventeen to realise he was gay. The fact that his mother had given him tickets for a Kylie Minogue concert for his birthday—and suggested he invite a rather nice young boy who worked at her hairdresser's to go along with him—should probably have given him a clue, too.

"Darling, you're our son and we love you unconditionally," she said, laying a kiss on the top of his head.

Giles sighed into her Chanel-scented bosom. "That's a yes, isn't it?"

"I'm afraid so, Giles. We've known for some time, but I think your father's still hoping it's just a phase and you'll grow out of it."

"You know, I always wondered why Daddy was so disappointed when it didn't work out between me and Ray from the salon," Giles said sadly. "I suppose this is why he doesn't like Hugh?"

"Darling, your father doesn't *dis*like Hugh," Mummy said, not quite looking him in the eye. "He just feels he hasn't been an awfully good influence on you, that's all."

Giles struggled to understand. "But Hugh's from one of the very best families. How can he possibly be a bad influence?"

Mummy sighed. "Hugh is, well…a little old-fashioned in his

attitudes. You know," she said brightly, pulling on the Cath Kidston oven gloves Giles had given her for Christmas, "I've never understood why you and Oz aren't a couple. After all, you get on marvellously."

Giles gave a nervous laugh. "Me? And Oz? You know we're just friends. I only met him last year, and Hugh and I were already together. So obviously, there's never been any question that we might, well…" He trailed off, because clearly there was no need to emphasize just how much Giles *hadn't* noticed how broad Oz's shoulders were, or the way his eyes crinkled up when he smiled. And Giles *certainly* hadn't ever sneaked a peek at his roommate doing sit-ups in his shorts first thing in the morning… "Anyway, he's never shown even the slightest sign of being interested in me that way," he finished, unable to keep a *soupçon* of disappointment out of his voice.

Mummy gave him a hug, and bent down to kiss him on the forehead. "I'm sure you know best, darling. Now, why don't you run along and play with your friend while I sort out lunch?"

Giles trudged dutifully into the living room. Oz was playing Little Big Planet, and his sackboy avatar seemed to have acquired a new costume, very much along Zorba the Greek lines. "*Et tu*, Oz?" Giles muttered, flopping onto the sofa.

"Uh?" Oz said, fingers flying on the console. He didn't look up from his game.

Giles crossed his legs, then uncrossed them. He picked up the *Radio Times* and stared, unseeing, at the cover before throwing it down again on the coffee table. The cushions seemed extraordinarily uncomfortable today. He leant forward. "I—" He stopped, and cleared his throat. "I thought I might go back and see her again," he said diffidently. "My mother, I mean. You could come too, if you like," he added.

Oz hit the pause button, and turned to face him. "Sure about that?"

"Yes. I want to show Angie I'm not embarrassed to have my friends meet her." Somehow, Giles had managed to twist himself into an extremely awkward position, but his limbs felt far too tense to try and relax.

"All right, then." Oz handed him the second console, and Giles took it, his breathing coming a little more easily. "Better leave it a few days, though, hadn't we? After all, it's been a lot for her to take in, too. But yeah, I'll look forward to meeting your mum."

Giles smiled. Suddenly he felt around ten stone lighter.

▲

ANGIE BEAMED WHEN she saw them the following week. "Wayne, love! I wasn't expecting to see you again so soon!" She turned to her daughter, who was sitting on the floor, fag in hand, filling out a sex survey in a magazine. "Didn't I say, Shards, that he wouldn't be round here again in a hurry, now he's found out what a bunch of bleedin' chavs we are?"

Giles felt a nasty twinge of guilt. "Of course I came round again!" he protested. "You're my mother! Oh—and this is Oz. He's a very good friend of mine." For some reason, Giles blushed as he said it. He flicked a glance at Oz, whose amused expression only made Giles's face grow hotter.

Angie gave him a hug. "Oh, it's all right, love. You can call him your boyfriend, nobody minds here."

The sack of potatoes in the armchair gave a grunt, which Giles suspected was Pete-speak for "snog him at your peril." The ape, thank God, was absent. Perhaps it'd been carted back to the zoo, Giles thought hopefully, then gave himself a mental slap on the wrist. "Really, Oz is just a friend," Giles insisted. "We share a house, that's all."

"Oh, get on with you! A good looking bloke like that? Well, if you don't want him, I'll 'ave him!" Angie cackled. "You 'ear that, Pete? I'm going to trade you in for a new model!"

"Hrrn," grunted Pete.

Oz looked terrified.

They sat down for a cup of tea. Giles was oddly touched to find his served in a mug with "Wayne" emblazoned on it in garish letters. "Well, i'n't this nice?" Angie said.

Giles opened his mouth to make a polite reply, but was interrupted by the slam of the front door. His brother, the ape, lumbered in, scratching its armpit. Its eyes narrowed when it saw them, and Giles instinctively huddled up to Oz for protection.

"'Ullo, love. Our Wayne's come round again, and he brung his boyfriend and all," Angie said brightly.

The ape scowled, and stepped towards them. Giles tensed.

Oz laughed, and leant back, resting one ankle on the opposite knee. His arms spread along the back of the sofa, emphasizing the breadth of his shoulders, while his shirt was stretched taut over a rather fine pair of pecs. "Nah, it's just your mum's little joke." Oz's voice sounded different, Giles realised. His vowels were flatter; the consonants less defined. "Not that you'd have a problem with it if I was, would you?" Despite his seemingly relaxed posture, Oz didn't take his eyes off Darren for an instant.

The ape stared at him for a long moment, then subsided, and slumped into its chair. After a brief tussle with its father for the remote control, which it lost, it settled for glaring steadily at the television and totally ignoring them.

"So have you got a bloke, then, love?" Angie asked brightly, as if massive amounts of testosterone had not just been expended in front of her.

"Oh, yes. His name's Hugh," Giles began, with a fond smile. "I met him in my first year at Oxford, at a wine tasting." He'd been instantly smitten by the man's rakish good looks, perfectly tailored jacket, and theatrical shudders of distaste at most of what was served. "We got talking over some rather vile champagne, and Hugh invited me to the Beaujolais breakfast over at his college, and well, we've been together ever since." He blushed a little at the memory of that morning. Hugh was reading Egyptology, which meant no lectures before noon—

and then only on Thursdays—and Giles had been only too happy to skip his own classes to accept Hugh's invitation to a post-breakfast rogering back at Merton.

"He sounds lovely, doesn't he, Shards? I hope he treats you right."

"Oh, Hugh's a perfect gentleman," Giles assured her. "We've had our ups and downs, but doesn't everyone?" Hugh hadn't spoken to him for *weeks* after Giles had been unwise enough to voice his opinion that the ban on foxhunting wasn't such a *very* bad idea, all things considered. Then there had been the business about Hugh sleeping with the captain of the Varsity rugby team before the try-outs. Giles had been devastated at first. But after Hugh's explanation, Giles had quite agreed it was simply the sensible thing to do—the rugger equivalent of the theatrical casting couch, so to speak—and nothing for him to be jealous about. "I'm seeing him tonight, actually—we're going to the opera."

"What about you, then, Oz?" Angie asked. "I bet you've got someone and all, with looks like those."

Oz started. "Oh, me? No, I'm—no. Not at the moment."

Giles wasn't sure he liked that "at the moment." Did Oz have someone he fancied, then? Who was he? And why hadn't Giles known about it? And who *was* he?

"Never mind, love," Angie consoled him. "I'm sure you'll find someone. 'Ere, Shards, you're not seeing no one at the mo, are you?"

Shards looked up from her article on STDs, and considered Oz for a long moment. "Nah. 'E ain't my type."

The ape wheezed.

"My loss, then," Oz said easily.

Giles was impressed by the way he managed to keep even the barest hint of sarcasm from his voice.

⚠

"ARE YOU SURE you're going to be all right if I go out tonight?" Giles fretted as they made their way back home. "I can't understand how Hugh managed to forget about your visit when he booked the tickets. It's not like him at all."

Oz gave a funny sort of laugh. "No, he's got a memory like an elephant, Hugh has," he said. "Don't worry about me. I'll be fine with your parents." He grinned suddenly. "Your mum said she'd get out your old baby photos to show me. And anyway, it's *La Bohème* tonight, isn't it? That's your favourite—you can't miss that." He hesitated for a moment, staring straight ahead. "But I think you should use the opportunity to tell Hugh about Angie. He's your boyfriend—he ought to know."

"He's not going to be pleased," Giles muttered darkly. "He doesn't even know I'm adopted."

Oz stared. "He has *met* your parents, hasn't he?"

Giles flushed. "I think he just assumes Mummy had a bit on the side. It seems to be almost *de rigueur* amongst his parents' set."

"Well, if he loves you," Oz said, "he'll accept you, whoever your parents are. Come on, you're still the same bloke you were yesterday, aren't you?"

"I suppose so," Giles said, brightening. Still, he couldn't help feeling a little queasy at the thought of telling Hugh about his birth mother.

⚓

GILES MET HUGH in the foyer at Covent Garden. They only just made it into the theatre in time—Hugh had been having drinks with some friends and just hadn't been able to get away—so they didn't get a chance to speak until later.

Not quite able to work up the courage to broach the subject of his parentage during the first interval, Giles listened instead to Hugh's scorn at the vocal capabilities of the mezzo-soprano (a rather pleasant-looking lady, Giles had thought, but he supposed that didn't really count for anything in opera). At the second interval, however, fortified by champagne, Giles forged ahead.

"Hugh, I'm adopted," he blurted out, inadvertently interrupting Hugh's amusing anecdote about how he'd got one over on one of his father's employees—but then, Giles *had* heard it twice already, so he had some excuse for not listening to Hugh as attentively as he otherwise would.

"Are you? Good Lord!" Hugh didn't look precisely pleased at the news.

Giles swallowed. "And I've found my birth mother. I've been round to see her twice now. She's married now, with two other children, and lives in Putney."

Hugh's lip curled in distaste. Then he gave a forced-sounding laugh. "Still, never mind. I'm sure you'll manage to lose her again."

"I don't want to lose her!" Giles protested. "It's not her fault she's working class, and lives in a council house."

"For God's sake, Giles," Hugh hissed. "Keep your voice down, will you? Surely you don't want everyone hearing about your sordid origins?"

"There's nothing sordid about my origins," Giles said stiffly. "Angie's a lovely lady."

"*Angie?*" There was a subtle change in Hugh's manner. "Giles...well, the fact is, I've been meaning to talk to you for some time. I don't think it's going to work out, you and me."

"*What?*" An icy chill suffused Giles's body, and it had nothing whatsoever to do with the champagne.

"And this only confirms it," Hugh continued. "I'm sure you'd be happier with someone of your own kind."

Giles bristled. "And what the hell is that supposed to mean?"

"Now, for God's sake don't go all *Socialist Worker* on me!"

"*Socialist Worker? Socialist* bloody *Worker?* What the hell are you on about?" Giles could hear his voice rising in both pitch and volume, but was powerless to prevent it.

"People of your class are always the same—"

"'Scuse me, gents," the barman broke in. "Would you mind

keeping it down a bit? People are starting to complain."

Giles swung round to face him. "Then they can damn well keep their noses out of it! This is a private discussion between me and my—Hugh? *Hugh*?" He looked around frantically, but Hugh had gone. Back to their box? Yes, that was it. Giles should go and join him, and by the end of the last act they'd be all right again.

When Giles got back to the box, it was empty. Reluctant to give up hope, Giles waited and waited. Mimi's death scene seemed even more affecting than usual, Giles wasn't sure why—he had tears streaming down his cheeks by the end. Hugh would mock him for it mercilessly—

But Hugh wasn't there.

▲

OZ WAS IN the conservatory again when Giles got home. He seemed to have forsaken the Insanely Bad Elf in favour of one of Mummy's bottles of Stoli. Giles slumped down beside him, and mutely held out his hand for the bottle of vodka.

"Hugh dumped me," he said, after a long swallow and a short coughing fit.

"Bastard. I'll scratch 'Upper Class Twat of the Year' into the side of his Merc with my keys, how about that?" Oz suggested.

Giles groaned, and took another swig from the bottle of vodka. "Wasn't it 'Twit', anyway? In the Monty Python sketch, I mean?"

"Oh, who cares. I think Hugh's more of a twat than a twit, don't you?"

Giles didn't answer. Was Hugh really a...what Oz had said? Had Giles just wasted nearly two years of his life on...on...a front bottom? And why was he drinking vodka, anyway? He looked around the conservatory, whose walls kept tilting drunkenly. Ha. Stupid walls. Couldn't hold their drink... "Where's my whisky?"

"Gone," Oz said happily, holding up not one but two empty bottles of Scotch.

On closer examination Giles realised that there were two Ozzes as well. "Bugger."

"Yeah, I could just scratch that into the car instead, that'd work. Be quicker, too. Less chance of getting caught. G'is the vodka."

Giles held out the bottle, wondering which of the two Ozzes would get to it first. The answer, as it happened, was neither.

"I think *I'll* take that, darling."

"Mummy?" Giles looked up and began to snigger. "I've got two mummies!" His face fell. "And no boyfriend," he finished dolefully.

"Oh, darling," Mummy sighed. "I'm so sorry. Do you want to talk about it?"

"'S all right, Mrs F. I'll look after him." Oz put a brawny arm around Giles's shoulder, the gesture of solidarity only slightly undermined by his explosive, eighty-proof belch in Giles's face.

Mummy smiled. In fact, both of her did. "In that case, I'll leave you boys to it. Now, I've brought you each a pint of water, so don't even think of going to bed before you drink it."

She left, and Oz took a swig of water. He gave another belch, this one slightly less flammable. "I've never thought Hugh was good enough for you. I was at school with him, you know."

"Oh?" Giles hiccupped. "Pardon me. He's never mentioned you being friends."

"Yeah, well, he wouldn't, would he? 'Cause we weren't. Catch him being matey with the scholarship boy," Oz added, his tone suddenly bitter.

Giles stared, as the words filtered through his befuddled brain. Oz's voice sounded different, too. Just like it had at Angie's.

"Yeah, that's right," Oz said, sticking his chin out. "I got in on a scholarship, 'cause no way could my mum and dad afford to send me to private school."

"Why are you talking funny?" Giles asked.

Oz laughed, but it wasn't a very happy sound. "I'm not. I've just stopped talking funny. See, you take a lad from a council estate and send him to some posh school, he's either going to start talking posh like the rest of them or get his bloody teeth kicked in. *This* is how I grew up talking." He stopped, and swigged some more water. "You know where I grew up? Not ten streets away from your real mum. The *chav.*" His arm slipped from around Giles's shoulder, and he sat rigidly, staring into the blackness of the garden.

Giles's head was spinning. "I don't—I think—" He lurched to a standing position. "I think I need to go to bed."

▲

NEXT MORNING, GILES woke up slumped face down on top of his bed, wearing only his shirt, which was bunched up under his armpits, and one sock. The cup of tea cooling by his bedside quelled any hopes that Mummy might not have been in and seen him in such a humiliating state.

Levering himself painfully upright, Giles drank the luke-warm, stewed tea. He dressed, and then staggered, shame-faced and heavy-headed, downstairs. Oz was sitting moodily at the kitchen table, glaring at a half-eaten slice of toast. Giles's stomach lurched in sympathy. "I've been a total arse, haven't I?" Giles said, taking a seat opposite his friend. They both winced as the chair scraped ear-splittingly on the terracotta tiles.

Oz gave him a weak smile. "Not a total arse. Half an arse, maybe. A single buttock." His voice was back to normal.

Giles wasn't sure he liked it. "You don't have to pretend to be posh for me," he said, trying to smile.

Oz shrugged. "Sometimes even I don't know which is my real accent any more." He gave a twisted smile. "So you're still speaking to me, now you know I'm a chav?"

"If you're still speaking to me," Giles said. He rested his

head in his hands. "I'm an idiot. A selfish, snobbish idiot. Who's been wasting his time with another selfish, snobbish idiot. And all this time you and I have been friends—sharing a house, even—and I didn't even bother to find out the first thing about you."

Oz was suddenly looking much more cheerful. He raised an eyebrow. "Yeah? You reckon? What's my favourite food?"

"Chinese, from the place down the road," Giles said immediately. "You like the sweet 'n sour pork balls and the deep fried crispy beef, but you think they're unhealthy so half the time you order chicken chow mein and monks' vegetables instead."

"Favourite film?"

"My Best Friend's Wedding, obviously."

"TV show?"

"*Being Human*, or anything else with Aidan Turner in it, because you fancy him like mad. Especially when he hasn't shaved recently." Giles blinked. "You know, at this rate, we could go on *Mr and Mrs*."

Oz laughed. "Exactly! That's just what I'm talking about—where you come from is only one part of you. It's who you really are that's important. That's something that wanker Hugh will never understand. You deserve more than to be some posh tosser's trophy boyfriend."

"What?" Giles stared. "Me? A trophy? But I'm just..."

"Just what?"

Giles sighed. "Short. Stupid. Snobbish. And hairier than an entire flange of gorillas."

Oz laughed again, and Giles gave him a hurt look. "You forgot to mention one thing."

"What?"

"You're also a bit of a berk sometimes. Okay, you're not the tallest bloke around, but you're gorgeous, and if you hadn't been brainwashed by that prick Hugh you'd know it."

Giles found he was blinking rapidly. "You think I'm gorgeous? Really?"

"'Course I do. And you're funny—all right, not always intentionally—and you really care about people, despite having spent the last couple of years in extremely bad company."

"I do?" Giles hadn't meant to say that out loud.

"Yes. You do." Oz hesitated, then stretched his hand across the table to cover Giles's. "Some of us were sort of hoping you might care about us in particular."

"They were? I mean, you were?" Still tussling with the third/second person problem, Giles's brain finally caught up to the import of what Oz had said. "You mean—"

"Yeah. Look, I know you're on the rebound from Hugh, and I'm not quite who you thought I was, but maybe, in a couple of months, if you're ready—"

Oz broke off abruptly as Giles launched himself across the table to silence his friend with a clumsy yet enthusiastic kiss. "I'm ready," he said fervently.

"Sure? Because—"

Feeling, in the circumstances, that actions spoke louder than words, Giles locked their lips together once more, and enthusiastically set about showing Oz just how very ready he was.

So what if they were a couple of chavs by birth? Giles knew good breeding when he saw it.

Or at least, he would do, just as soon as their hangovers wore off.

▲

About JL Merrow

JL MERROW IS that rare beast: an English person who refuses to drink tea. Having grown up by the seaside, she also loathes fish and chips. She read Natural Sciences at Cambridge, where she learned many things, chief amongst which was that she never wanted to see the inside of a lab ever again. Her one regret is that she never mastered the ability of punting one-handed whilst holding a glass of champagne.

She writes across genres, with a preference for contemporaries and the paranormal, and is frequently accused of humour.

Website (including free reads section): jlmerrow.com
Blog: jl-merrow.livejournal.com
Facebook: facebook.com/jl.merrow
Goodreads: goodreads.com/author/show/2980235.J_L_Merrow

A Naughty Trip
by Serena Yates

AUTHOR'S NOTE: This story is set right before the beginning of *Discovering the Actor (New Horizons, #2)*.

▲

"JUST WAIT TILL we're in the air." Scott squeezed Anton's hand gently, loving the shiver which ran through the man's entire body at those words. The sexy research librarian was the most sensitive lover he'd ever had.

"I can't wait till we're *there*." Anton turned his head away from the waiting lounge's busy bar. His sky blue eyes were twinkling, good humour clearly winning over grumpiness about the five-hour flight already behind them.

"Oh, but you have no idea what I have planned for your in-flight entertainment on the next leg of our trip." Scott gave Anton his most provocative wink. He'd booked them business class for the second leg of their journey from Los Angeles to Edinburgh, wanting to make the flight from Newark to Scotland memorable in more ways than one.

"My own personal entertainment?" Anton's eyebrows rose.

"Extremely personal." Scott winked. "Have you heard of the Mile High Club?"

"Scott!" Anton looked too cute when he tried for indignant.

"Anton?" Scott feigned innocence, knowing full well that his lover was on to him. He'd only recently given up a career as a gay porn star, so *innocent* was one of the least likely images for Scott to project. Not only that, but since he'd got together with Anton they'd constantly tried to outdo each other in coming up with the most deliciously naughty plans for sex in exciting places. That, Scott had found over the last month since meeting Anton at the Komlos Foundation's Santa Barbara branch, was half the fun of having an intelligent partner.

"Really!" Anton put his 'prim and proper' librarian's face on, except it didn't work half as well without the reading glasses.

"What?" Scott only barely held back the grin that wanted to emerge. He'd had no idea acting classes would come in handy when joking around with his lover.

"You can't be serious! That's probably illegal." Anton shook his head, making his strawberry blond curls bounce.

Scott wished he could slide his hand into them, pull Anton closer and kiss him for hours. Unfortunately, behaving that way in public was not going to go down well with the authorities. He'd have to wait till he was able to make love to Anton in the air. Just thinking about it had him half hard. Shit. Walking onto their plane with a hard on was not going to be easy or much fun.

"I'm totally serious. And so what if it's illegal?" Scott entwined their fingers. "Making love on the beach like we did after we'd only just met was not entirely within the limits of the law, either—nor was that time in your office."

"Okay, okay, I get it." Anton blushed and pushed his slightly-too-long hair off his fine-boned face. "But do you have to talk about it like this? Someone could hear."

"I'll talk about it because I know it makes you hot." Scott glanced at his lover's groin, where a significant bulge was trying to push its way past the zipper.

"Shit." Anton put a hand over the unruly part of his anatomy as his hips jerked the tiniest amount. "I really, really don't want to come in my pants right now."

"Why not? It's a new location for us, and we do have a couple of spare sets of clothing in our hand luggage." Scott, having experienced lost luggage a few times too often, had insisted they come prepared. He didn't really want to come in his pants, either—they'd more than done their share of that during the first week after meeting, and even a couple of times since then. But it was such fun to tease Anton.

"Well…" Anton's gaze turned calculating as he looked up and down Scott's increasingly aroused body.

Scott groaned. Anton was getting good at returning the favour of building sexual tension between them. It was going to be a very long layover. The boarding procedures would probably kill him, and who knew how long it would be before take-off and for the seatbelt signs to be switched off?

"Now look what you've done." Scott discreetly pointed at his groin. A full erection was now attempting to tent his well-worn jeans. Not for the first time, he wondered whether excessive libido had been the reason for his forefathers to invent and wear kilts. He might not be a Highlander, but he could wear a kilt as well as the next Scottish man. He'd left his behind when he'd moved out of his parents' house ten years ago, but now that he was returning, maybe it was time to start wearing one again? Especially with Anton around.

"It's only fair." Anton's grin was wide enough to split his face. "And anyway, what are the washrooms for?"

"Oh, my God. I've created a monster." Scott's arousal was growing by the minute and he was going to blow any second now.

"Just trying to keep up with you." Anton leant towards him. "You may be a former gay porn star, but I bet you've never done it in a bathroom stall at an airport."

"Fuck!" Scott gripped the edge of his seat with his free hand and bit the inside of his cheek to regain control over his raging libido. He was not going to come in the lounge, giving all those serious, business types in stuffy suits a show. Even a bathroom stall was better than that.

"Indeed." Anton leant back in his seat, a triumphant grin playing around his deep-red lips. In fact, the rest of his face was approaching that colour as well. Small beads of sweat stood on his high forehead, and his hand trembled against Scott's fingers.

"That's it." Scott rose on shaky legs, pulling Anton with him then grabbed their small rolling suitcase. "You're coming with me."

"I certainly won't be coming much after you." Anton's voice was low enough that only Scott would hear.

Scott laughed. He loved Anton's sense of humour.

▲

ANTON FOLLOWED A very determined Scott in a complete haze of lust. He vaguely sensed some surprised looks from the other passengers, but his lover was all he could focus on. The man was a master at driving him to distraction with lust, then making him come harder than he ever had in his, admittedly somewhat boring, life before Scott. It looked as if today was going to be no exception. Trip or no trip, they were apparently going to have sex. Three times, counting the morning blow jobs they'd given each other and if he was lucky and Scott was going to keep his promise of making love while in the air.

But, first things first.

Anton followed Scott into the luxurious executive bathroom, black faux marble and gleaming, imitation gold faucets included, glancing left and right while Scott decided where they should go. He normally wasn't one to follow, but with Scott it felt right. His lover had never given him the feeling of being weak because he occasionally liked to do as he was told. Anton had been a lot less experienced than Scott when they'd first met, but he was catching up quickly. At this rate, he'd try to turn the tables one of these days, see if Scott might like that.

Not now, though. He was too far gone for any type of finesse. Luckily, his lover was the decisive type and steered them towards the shower cubicles at the back, along a line so straight it would have done a mathematician proud.

"Come on." The impatience in Scott's voice as he pulled Anton into the generously-sized and appointed cubicle was gratifying.

Anton barely had time to grab one of the towels from the small table at the entrance to the separate shower area before he was pulled into the cubicle on the right. He found himself smashed up against the closed door, his back pressed to the wooden surface, while his front was deliciously assaulted by Scott's hard body. Touching in all the right places before they even got started, he pushed back against Scott's hips grinding into his as he opened his mouth to receive his lover's passionate kiss.

Scott's hands framed Anton's face to hold him still. Soft lips were followed by a hot tongue that met his for a thorough 'hello' and 'glad to see you'. Anton brought his hands to Scott's ass, making sure his lover stayed as close as possible.

"Naked." Scott had pulled back. His blue eyes were a few shades darker than normal, more than one strand of hair had escaped the otherwise neat ponytail he wore, and the muscular chest was heaving about as much as Anton's own.

Anton nodded, sliding his hands around to Scott's front to fumble his lover's button and zipper open. Before he knew it, Scott had done the same to him and now held Anton's throbbing cock in his hand. Tightening his grip, Scott started to stroke, and Anton almost lost it. With the last bit of focus he had left, he pulled Scott's leaking cock out of its hiding place, made a tunnel with his hand and returned the favour.

Holding on to Scott's hip with his free hand, all he could do was squeeze the other around Scott's cock, hoping it would be enough. Scott's hand on his own cock certainly felt more than sufficient. Helpless to resist the need to thrust, he soon fucked Scott's hand with abandon, throwing his head back and closing his eyes because the friction felt so good.

Scott buried his face in Anton's neck, the sudden sucking

on the sensitive area driving Anton over the edge. Hot semen shot from the tip of his cock as he emptied his balls.

"Fuck." Scott stilled and an answering spurt of heat added to the mess they'd created.

Scott lifted his head and kissed Anton again. This kiss was slower, one of sated bliss and shared release rather than the one of hard passion they'd exchanged earlier.

"Maybe now I can hold on until they switch off the seatbelt signs." Scott gave him another kiss. "That's a big 'maybe', though. Just look at how sexy you are with that 'I've just come' grin on your face. I'm certainly ready to go again."

"You're always ready to go again." Anton smiled as he pushed one of the loose strands of hair off Scott's face. "Not that I'm complaining, but in this case, I think we have about five minutes to clean up, make ourselves presentable and get to our gate."

Scott looked at his watch.

"Shit, you're right." Scott pulled back, reluctance showing in every slow movement he made. "It's a good thing we took the edge off, though—I don't think I could have made it without this little interlude."

"Same here." Anton chuckled as he started wiping their hands, before creating enough space to allow them to put their clothing back together.

He was proud they hadn't even needed the spare clothes after all. Then again, their trip was far from over and the Mile High Club was still beckoning. When they were dressed, they made their way outside and towards the gate. It was hard to focus on the reality of checking in when all he really wanted to do was focus on the naughty images passing before his inner eye. Anton shook his head at his own audacity. He couldn't believe he was seriously considering breaking the law by having sex on a plane.

Five weeks ago, before Scott had walked into his office at the Komlos Foundation because he wanted to learn about being a research librarian so he could audition for a role in a movie, Anton had been painfully shy. His experience with boyfriends had been limited, to say the least. After the last loser, he'd decided he wouldn't bother anymore.

Scott had changed everything, from building his professional confidence to increasing his enjoyment of sex. It looked as if his lover was about to take it to the next level.

Anton couldn't wait.

▲

"HERE YOU ARE, gentlemen, seats 3A and 3B are all yours." The young steward had openly ogled Scott since they'd boarded the plane.

Scott had felt flattered at first, an automatic reaction left over from his days as a gay porn star. But seeing Anton throw furtive glances at the steward and withdraw into himself had made Scott realise how insecure his lover still was. He was going to work extra hard at helping him lose any doubts he was the only man Scott was even remotely interested in. Even though Anton had agreed to 'have him' when Scott had asked to make their liaison more permanent, they'd never talked about it, never really formalised it. Maybe it was time to correct that oversight. Anton would probably appreciate it.

Scott let Anton have the window seat, wanting him to have a good view when they landed in Edinburgh just under seven hours from now. He thanked the steward but didn't smile, sat down, fastened the seatbelt and grabbed Anton's hand as soon as the steward was gone. Looking deep into Anton's eyes, he bent close enough to whisper.

"It's you I want to make love to as soon as we're allowed to leave our seats, not the airline twink." Scott followed his statement with a slow lick of Anton's earlobe, just to make sure the other man got the message.

"It is, huh?" Anton took a deep breath. "I shouldn't be so

insecure, should I? I know it's not logical, but I can't help it. You're so gorgeous, everyone wants you, and I'm just—well, I'm just me."

"There's no 'just' about you." Scott smiled and squeezed Anton's fingers. "Just remember that."

"It'll take some time." Anton sighed.

"Maybe what you need is an official title." Scott pretended to frown in thought.

"And what might that be?" Anton's lips twitched.

"Oh, I don't know. I believe I offered you three when we first decided to stay together. There was 'lover' and 'boyfriend'. There's always 'partner', if you prefer?" Scott held his breath, hoping Anton might finally be ready to put their commitment into words.

"You—I—you're serious?" Anton's eyes widened.

"Very!"

"Well, I'm already your lover, so that wouldn't work. And people can have more than one lover, anyway. 'Partner' sounds a bit too formal." Anton swallowed. And I kind of like 'boyfriend', anyway."

"Boyfriend it is." Scott winked. "And guess who will be the first to find out?"

Just then the steward came back, offering them champagne, orange juice or water. They each picked a small glass of champagne. Scott looked up at the young man, who'd started staring at him again. Shit, maybe he'd seen him in one of his movies?

"Thank you for the champagne. This way my boyfriend and I will be able to toast our trip in style." Scott lifted his glass then turned to Anton. "Thanks for saying yes to meeting my parents."

Anton blushed furiously, but his smile was back to normal.

"Meeting your parents?" The steward sounded surprised. "Must be serious, then."

"Oh, yes, very." Anton got into the spirit of things. "And I'm the jealous type, just in case you were wondering."

"I—I wasn't." The steward cleared his throat. "Well, I wish

you a good flight, then. Please let me know if there's anything I can get you."

Scott waited a few beats to make sure the steward was gone. "I meant that. Here's to us officially being boyfriends." He clinked glasses with Anton.

"I'm glad." Anton took a sip of his champagne. His gaze turned devious. "So, that means we get to join the Mile High Club twice, right?"

"Twice? I like the sound of that." Scott hadn't planned on two rounds, but, hey, he was flexible.

"No, not that way." Anton laughed. "I just meant we get to join as lovers and as boyfriends."

"I like my interpretation better." Scott grinned.

"I bet you do." Anton rolled his eyes. "So does my cock."

Scott almost lost the champagne he'd been about to swallow. Anton was nothing if not full of surprises. He'd also made sure Scott was well on his way to an erection. Way to go, with at least half an hour of safety announcements, a long taxi before takeoff and potentially endless minutes of ascending towards their travel height.

By the time they were allowed to undo their seatbelts, Scott was painfully hard. He looked around, but the other passengers were busy reading their newspapers, pulling out their laptops or fiddling with their earphones. The stewards and stewardesses were nowhere to be seen, probably busy preparing dinner.

It was now or never.

"I'll take the door on the left. Give me two minutes then follow me." Scott rose from his seat, patting his back pocket to make sure the lube and condom were still in place. Anton had blushed when he'd seen him transfer the sachet from their little transparent plastic bag of cosmetics to his pants pocket.

Scott made it into the toilet in record time, leaving the door a tiny bit ajar, as people might get suspicious if Anton approached a locked room. He took the time while waiting for his lover to look around, trying to work out the best way to do what he had in mind. Even though there was a little more space than in economy, it was going to be a very tight fit.

Anton squeezed himself inside only minutes later. He locked the door and turned around, tilting his head up for a kiss. Scott gladly complied and dived into Anton's hot mouth with all the passion he felt for his newly-minted boyfriend. Kissing Anton to within an inch of his life had become his new favourite hobby. Scott leant against the wall and pulled Anton closer. Sliding his hands around, he opened his lover's pants and slid them down his legs, then grabbed the sachet and condom from his own pants before letting them slide down as well.

"Are you sure this is going to work?" Anton looked sceptical.

"Sure." Scott grinned as he opened the foil packet and sheathed his straining erection before pulling out the second packet and giving Anton's hard cock the same treatment. There was no point in making a bigger mess than necessary. "But you're going to have to turn around..."

▲

ANTON WAS SURE they wouldn't have much time before someone discovered them. How embarrassing would that be? Strangely enough, the thought made him even hotter and he quickly did as Scott had asked. He gripped the wash basin, spread his legs as far as possible and lifted his ass. God, he felt like such a slut. But ever since Scot had told him about his plans, he'd wanted this with an intensity that surprised him. Even the little episode in the airport's bathroom stall hadn't really cooled him down. The gesture of covering him with a second condom was so thoughtful it made him fall a little more for Scott.

"I love it when you do that." Scott's warm hands landed on his hips.

"What? Offer myself to you?" He turned his head around to look at his boyfriend. "You don't think it's too slutty?"

"Nothing you and I do is slutty." Scott stroked one ass

cheek while his other hand vanished. Hopefully to get the lube.
"Or everything is. Either way, we're equals in this. I want you as
much as it looks like you want me."

"Thank God for that." He went to the tips of his toes as
the first touch of a slightly cool, slippery finger touched his
hole. "Yes!"

"Sorry about the speed, but I don't think we have very long
until that steward, or someone else, will discover we're both
gone but only one toilet is locked." Scott slid his first finger into
Anton's waiting ass.

"More. Please." He always wanted more, and today it was
particularly urgent, for many reasons.

Luckily, the first finger was quickly followed by a second.
Scott finger-fucked him so well, Anton could probably come
from that alone. Within moments he was pushing back, trying to
get more of the digits inside him. All his nerve endings were sen-
sitised, his hole felt empty and wanted more, and he really didn't
want to come before Scott was inside him. He wasn't even sure
that would make them full members of the Mile High Club.

"Please, Scott, fuck me." He ground his teeth to stop himself from screaming. "Need you. Now."

He almost howled when Scott entered him in one sure
stroke, just like he wanted. The angle was different from anything they'd tried so far—Anton's channel was much tighter
than normal because he couldn't spread his feet all that much,
and the additional excitement of the location drove him to the
edge more quickly than he'd thought possible.

Scott lifted Anton's left leg until his knee was as high up as
it would go. Then he pulled out and thrust back in with such
force the wall shook. Anton balled his fist and bit into it to stop
his screams from emerging as Scott bent closer, slid a hand
around his stomach and started pummelling his ass in earnest.

Scott's closeness, feeling his powerful thrusts inside him
and seeing his face in the mirror when Anton looked up, was
too much. With a barely-muffled whimper, he started coming

into his condom. Pleasure racked his body as the orgasm raced up his spine, his ass clenching in delight.

Scott was right behind him. Biting into Anton's shoulder, he shuddered through his orgasm. His grip tightened and Anton almost came again as he felt his boyfriend tremble with his orgasm. He couldn't wait for them to get tested so they could forget about the condoms. He already knew Scott was it for him, and it was beginning to look as if that was mutual.

"That was amazing." Scott pulled out and dealt with his condom while Anton was still trying to recover. "Welcome to one of the most exclusive clubs in the world."

"Definitely one of the most fun." Anton shook his head to get rid of the lust-filled fog and disposed of his condom before starting the contortions needed to get dressed again. One look in the mirror showed him all hope for his hair was lost. He'd need to bring a brush for his next visit to the bathroom.

"I like your hair when it's so tousled." Scott slid one of his big hands through the unruly curls.

"At least one of us does." Anton grinned.

Scott left first, Anton following a few minutes later. The steward's knowing grin when he served their dinner made Anton blush. But it had been so worth it. Cuddling up to Scott after dinner, he spread a blanket over both of them so they could get some sleep. It was going to be a short night, but the biggest adventure of his life waited at the other end.

Anton couldn't wait to land in Edinburgh and start exploring his new home. He could only hope the rest of his stay was going to be as naughty as this trip. But with Scott, his new boyfriend, at his side, that was not going to be a problem.

He yawned and closed his eyes.

Scotland, here I come!

⋀

About Serena Yates

SERENA YATES IS a night owl who has loved reading all her life, and is now a full-time writer. Male/male romance is her passion, and her work ranges from the romantic to the erotic, from short stories to novels. Whether the story setting is contemporary, sci-fi or paranormal, she guarantees a happy ending.

Website: serenayates.com
Facebook: facebook.com/serenaequalityyates
Twitter: @serenayates
Goodreads: goodreads.com/author/show2964333.Serena_Yates
Email: serenayates09@googlemail.com

Beside the Seaside
by Lucy Felthouse

I WAS SO engrossed in staring at the designs in the window of the tattoo parlour that I almost jumped out of my skin when the door was pulled open and a girl stepped out onto the pavement beside me.

My face must have expressed my shock because she looked at me, smiling, and said "Are you okay?"

"I'm fine," I replied, noting immediately how cute she was. "You just startled me, that's all. I was miles away."

She motioned towards the window. "You thinking of getting one?"

I shrugged. "Yeah, maybe. I've been toying with the idea for a while, but I've just never gotten round to it. Did you just get one?"

"Not this time, no. I was just popping in to let Steve know how pleased I was with my piercing. It's all healed up great."

"Your piercing?" My eyebrows raised of their own accord as I studied her and saw none, bar the ones in her ears, which looked like they'd been there for some time.

Grinning wickedly, she then stuck out her tongue. With her short dark hair and cheeky dimples, the expression made her look like a mischievous pixie. A hot mischievous pixie.

"Oh, wow!" I said, trying not to think about how sexy the

piercing looked on her. "That's so cool. And you're so brave. I'd never have the guts to get that done."

"Why not?" she asked. "You're obviously not that scared of pain if you're considering a tattoo."

"I know but I'd worry that something would go wrong with it. And don't you have to stay off solid food for a while afterwards?" I was horrified at the thought of not being able to eat my favourite foods for weeks on end. I'd waste away.

"You do. But I have the all clear now, so I can eat what I damn well want. Which is why I'm about to treat myself to some fish and chips." She looked me up and down, as if assessing my suitability. "Wanna come?"

"Sure," I found myself saying, "sounds great."

I turned and followed her as she headed towards the sea front. I frowned. It wasn't like me to start chatting to random strangers, let alone to go off with them. I told myself it wasn't just because I found her attractive, but I couldn't convince even my own brain. She didn't look like a serial killer or a psycho, so I was sure I'd be okay. Plus, she was smaller than me. I could probably take her, anyway.

I laughed aloud as another thought occurred to me.

"What's tickled your funny bone?" she said, turning to me, a smile quirking the corners of her mouth.

"I just realised we're going off for lunch together, but I don't even know your name!"

She slapped her forehead theatrically.

"Sorry, babe," she said, holding her hand out formally. "I'm Candy."

Shaking her hand, I replied, "I'm Ella. Nice to meet you."

"Okay," she said, dropping her hand back to her side, "now that's out of the way, let's get something to eat. I'm fucking starving."

Candy picked up her pace, marching purposefully towards the nearest fish and chip shop. I presumed she'd chosen it for its proximity, because the shop with the best reputation was up on the High Street. Mind you, it was always packed full of tourists, so maybe she was avoiding it on purpose. I didn't care either way. Soon after Candy had mentioned food, I'd remembered that I hadn't eaten yet, and my stomach had quickly emphasised that fact, grumbling away as we walked.

Scurrying after her, I took the time to appreciate Candy's rear view. She was wearing jeans that hung low on her hips and a little T-shirt, and I could see that she was tattooed as well as pierced. A design adorned her lower back, all swirls and loops, and I thought about how nice it would be to trace the pattern with my tongue. I'd love to tease her until she writhed beneath me.

Candy turned to make sure I was keeping up, and I quickly flicked my gaze up to hers. The twinkle in her eye made me think she'd caught me out, but she didn't say anything. Perhaps she didn't mind?

A few minutes later we had trays of delicious-smelling fish and chips in our hands. I looked around for somewhere we could sit. There was an empty bench nearby that would do nicely. But before I could point it out, Candy piped up, "Come with me."

It wasn't a question. She'd stomped off before I got a chance to react and I ended up trailing after her like a little lost puppy.

She was heading along the promenade towards the row of brightly coloured beach huts that delighted tourists all year round. Of course, living locally, I'd never needed to use one. I could scuttle home from the beach and hit the shower in ten minutes flat. This was clearly not the case with Candy as, once we reached the end of the row, she rummaged around in her pocket.

Bringing out a key, she grinned at me. "Wanna guess which one is mine?"

Looking at the wooden huts, I wondered if it was a trick question. They were all painted in pretty pastel colours, but that was it. None had any defining features, other than a unique number to identify them.

Candy nudged me playfully, almost causing me to drop my lunch on the floor.

"I'm just messing with ya," she said. "You'd never guess. If it was up to me, I'd have whacked jazzy patterns or something on ours. But they've all gotta stay uniform, or summat. My grandad'd kill me if I did anything. It's his really, you see, but he lets us all use it pretty much when we want."

"Oh." I said, my brain having lost the ability to think of anything more intelligent or interesting to say. I needn't have worried; Candy was plenty chatty enough for us both.

"Hold these," she said, handing me her parcel of food. "This lock's a bugger."

She proceeded to wrestle with the padlock on the door of the very first beach hut, which was painted in a lovely pale blue colour. After some grunting and the occasional expletive, Candy finally waved the padlock triumphantly in my face.

Flinging open the doors, she said, "Welcome to my humble abode."

Candy's granddad was obviously a meticulous person. There wasn't much in the tiny hut, but everything had its place. Retrieving a deck chair from a hook on the wall, Candy erected it and gestured grandly at me to sit down. I laughed and plopped into the chair.

"Why, thank you, young lady," I said.

She put up her own chair which, in the limited space, ended up just millimetres from mine. "I'm no lady," she giggled, "who told you that? Now gimme them chips."

I handed them over. We both unwrapped our food and ate in silence, staring out to the rolling and tossing waves.

Soon enough, the noise of rustling flicked my attention back to Candy. She'd finished. Looking into her tray, I saw she'd eaten the lot. I wondered how on Earth she stayed so skinny if she ate like that all the time. Tossing the rubbish onto the table behind us, she stretched contentedly and said, "They were fucking lovely. Beats soup and rice pudding, eh?"

I remembered then that she'd been on liquids for weeks. No wonder she'd wolfed her lunch down like it was going out of fashion.

"Absolutely. You want any more?" I asked, tilting my not quite empty tray at her.

"No, I've had enough now, thanks. You done?"

I nodded. Reaching behind her, Candy retrieved her rubbish then held out her hand for mine. I handed it to her, and she stood up and sashayed out of the hut to a nearby bin. Depositing our litter, she dusted off her hands. I grinned at her, and she beamed back.

"Feel better?" I asked as she settled back into the chair next to me.

"Oh, yeah. My first proper meal as a pierced woman. Delish."

"So it was okay? It didn't catch on stuff?"

"Nah," she said, shaking her head. "I knew it wouldn't. I did my research before I had it done."

"Oh, right." I said, again left with nothing interesting to say.

"You know what else I found out?" Candy continued even as I shook my head. "It's meant to be really good for oral sex."

I made a strange noise somewhere between a laugh and a squeal.

She looked at me, one eyebrow raised. "How would you like to find out?"

I merely stared at her, a rabbit trapped in headlights. She was deadly serious. I glanced out the front of the hut then looked back at Candy. I opened my mouth, but she cut me off.

"I'll close the doors."

I wanted her, there was no question of it. I'd found her attractive from the very moment we met. I just hadn't realised she felt the same.

Candy raised both eyebrows now, an exasperated expression crossing her face.

"Well?" She poked out her tongue and wiggled it at me obscenely.

I moved uncomfortably in my chair, already becoming wet. I nodded. "Shut the doors."

Some time later, as we both slumped, sated, sweaty and exhausted in the deck chairs, I came to the conclusion that her research had been absolutely correct. I'd never come so hard in my life. Until she did it again, that was.

▲

About Lucy Felthouse

LUCY FELTHOUSE STUDIED Creative Writing at University. Whilst there, she was dared to write an erotic story—so she did. It went down a storm and she's never looked back. Lucy has had stories published by Cleis Press, Noble Romance, Ravenous Romance and Xcite Books

Website: lucyfelthouse.co.uk
Twitter: @cw1985
Facebook: facebook.com/lucyfelthousewriter

Fighting Cocks
by Stevie Woods

Wiltshire 1595

"PETER, WHY MUST you disobey me?"

"Mother, please." Peter closed his eyes. *Not another lecture please.* His hand dropped from the door handle and he turned to face his mother.

"Why must you spend so much time with the tavern-keeper's son?" His mother went on as if he had never spoken. "He is not worthy of you, he brings you into disrepute."

"He's a good friend. The only real friend I have, and you know he's not just a simple tavern-keeper's son. It is not easy being in charge, you know. Father was always telling me I wasn't ready and then he just goes and dies with no warning."

"Peter Anston!"

Peter sighed. "*Jesu!* I did not mean to sound harsh. But you know what he was like. He kept everything close to his chest."

"All the more reason for you to learn how to run the farms and not leave so much to me and Landers. Going gallivanting all round the countryside with Norman Early is no way to behave. You should—"

"Mother, stop! I do not require your advice. I am old enough to know what I want, whose company I wish to share."

"I bemoan the day your father died," she said, emotion lacing her voice. She lifted watery eyes to him. "If he were still here you would not behave like this. He gave his whole life to his land, and you would let it all go to wrack and ruin."

"Do not exaggerate so," Peter said with a sigh. "It is in the tenant farmers' interest to work the land well and they pay their rents on time." His mother raised an eyebrow, so he quickly added, "Mostly. I went to see Ryson when you demanded, didn't I? He paid his back rents, didn't he?"

"Ay, but I shouldn't have had to remind you twice about that. A good landowner would know such things. Your father was always looking ahead, planning, building for the future. He chose men to work for him who had good heads on their shoulders, who could turn their hands to more than duty. If it wasn't for Landers—"

"But we do have Landers, Mother, and you know we can rely on him, he is almost like one of the family," Peter interrupted with a touch of asperity. Taking a breath to calm his rising anger, Peter said more calmly, "I am but eighteen summers, Mother. Life is meant to be lived." Before she said anything else he quickly opened the door and stepped out. He heard her call after him but he ignored her—and the rising anger in her voice.

Jesu! He too bemoaned his father's death. He'd loved his father, but the truth was he had been in the powerful man's shadow all his life. He had blossomed in the freedom suddenly opened to him. Deep inside he knew his mother was right, he was not doing his duty by her, but somehow just now it didn't matter. There would be time enough for that when he had his fill of freedom. All that mattered now was that he needed to see Norman.

Peter smiled as he thought of Norman. The tavern-keeper's wayward son was two years older than Peter and yet somehow he seemed even older than that compared to Peter who had always been under his father's thumb, the dutiful son.

Norman had taunted Peter over the previous year or so and

yet somehow there was always good humour under the insults and jibes. One evening, shortly after his father had died, Peter had had too much to drink and had bumped into Norman as he staggered away from the Fighting Cocks Tavern. Norman had laughed at him, joked at his inability to hold his ale. This time Peter wasn't going to take it and he had taken a swing at Norman. However, he had not only missed his mark but had fallen against Norman in the process. Laughing, Norman had caught him and held him closely against his body.

"Hold there, Peter," Norman had said.

"Master Peter!" he had stated, the demand being somewhat spoiled by his slurring the words. "You will…will show me respect."

"Oh, I think not," Norman had replied. "A man has to earn the right to respect. And you have not."

There had been something hard and unyielding in Norman's words and in the look in his eye. Peter had stared at him and felt the stirring in his belly that he usually only experienced alone in his bed at night. He had felt embarrassed and ducked his head. Norman had set him more firmly on his feet, but he didn't move away.

"Peter?" Norman had asked. "Peter, look at me."

Peter had felt impelled to answer the demand in Norman's voice and he raised his eyes. He had half expected Norman to be angry and then suddenly, through the haze of his intoxication, he had remembered his position.

"How…how dare—" Peter had hiccupped, "dare you speak to me like that!" It was not Norman's place to take him to task. Peter had stepped back a little and stared at Norman, ready to…Whatever he had been thinking faded away at the look in Norman's eyes.

"You feel it too, don't you?" Norman had asked softly. Peter had licked his lips but no words had come . "I have watched you," Norman went on. "You have never looked at the girls in the village; indeed, you've hardly seemed to notice those who looked at you." Norman had smiled.

Peter had opened his mouth, closed it again as he tried to gather his thoughts. He tried again. "Feel it?" he had queried.

Norman had pressed closer, and Peter had felt the pressure of Norman's groin against his thigh and had gasped at the hardness he felt there. Colour had flooded his cheeks as he felt his own prick rise in response and Norman had laughed softly. "Oh yes," Norman had said, "You feel it."

"I don't…I. Oh my!" Norman had pressed against him again and suddenly Peter's prick wanted to be free of its restraint.

"Come," Norman had said. "I know just the place."

Peter had been too bemused, too drunk, to do anything other than to follow Norman's lead. And that night, in a small barn half way between the tavern and his home, Peter learned what it was like to rut with a man. He hadn't even known until that night that that was what he really wanted, but he couldn't deny the heat and the pleasure that had flooded his being as Norman had taken both their naked pricks in his hand and had brought Peter to his first completion by a hand other than his own.

Neither could Peter deny the dreams that he'd always thought were only the confused ramblings of a tired mind. In those dreams, Peter had never quite been able to recognise who he was with, only that it had been a dark shadowy figure. A figure that had always managed to hold him down, to drive him crazy. Yet there had never been penetration in his dreams the way there should have been with a woman.

Now he understood; his body had known what he wanted before his mind could accept the truth. Peter did not want women, he wanted men. *Jesu!* He was a sodomite. He should have felt revulsion, shame, but all he felt was relief that finally he knew who he was.

He had met with Norman many times since that first night and Norman had shown him much more, including initiating him into the act of sodomy itself. Peter could still remember that first time as clear as day, and he guessed he always would. It hadn't been easy, but it had been fulfilling in so many ways. The way Norman had touched him and made him feel so alive. Just brushes of Norman's fingers over his skin had sent tendrils of fire through his body. The way Norman's eyes had lit up as he held Peter's gaze. The weight of Norman's body draped over his, the slide of the oil between his buttocks, the pressure of Norman's fingers inside his passage. The pain that had turned to pleasure as Norman had pushed his thick prick inside him. The sound of his own whimpers in his ears as Norman had thrust into him over and over. Norman's gasp as he had climaxed deep inside Peter.

⚓

PETER ARRIVED AT the Fighting Cocks Tavern a few minutes late. The tavern was more than its simple name implied; it was one of the designated places on the main road between London and Bath where horses could be changed and where passengers could obtain a good room for the night. Mr. Early had done well enough that he had increased the size of the tavern two years earlier. Peter looked around and, as usual, Norman was helping his father to serve the customers. Norman smiled as he saw Peter before going to the serving hatch and pulling off his apron. He went to get his coat but as he approached Peter, Norman's father intercepted him.

Keeping his voice low, Norman's father said, "Where do you think you are going? We are busy tonight and I need your help." It was obvious that Mr. Early had meant to keep the conversation private, but Peter had chosen a quiet corner to wait and his hearing was good enough that he could pick up each word.

"But I have plans for tonight."

"Not tonight. I need you here. The whores will wait," he added with a curl of his lip. Mr. Early had the same opinion as Peter's mother as to what Norman and Peter got up to when they went off together, and it was so much easier, and safer, to let them believe the lie. The truth was so much more dangerous.

"It is my night off," Norman said.

"You get a night off when I say so," Mr. Early said sharply. "You know Walter is home sick."

"That's not my fault!" Norman declared.

"No, but it is your responsibility. You want to take over this place when the time comes, you need to earn it!"

"Father," Norman began and Peter knew what he would say next, how he would promise that he would work twice as hard and long the next day. The thing was, his father knew it too.

"No, Norman," Mr. Early interrupted and Norman froze, his mouth half open. Mr. Early looked steadily at Norman before he added, "You leave here now and you need not bother coming back."

For once Norman was speechless. He just stood and stared at his father and then without a word walked back to the serving hatch and picked up his apron. Peter watched him go; Mr. Early was usually an easy-going man, but when he reached his limit there was no gainsaying him.

Peter moved from the corner and sat at a nearby empty table. After a moment Mr. Early walked up.

"You want a drink, Master Anston?" he asked, interrupting Peter's thoughts and Peter nodded. Mr. Early's tone was polite but Peter couldn't mistake the look of resentment in his eyes.

Norman was in a mood all night because things had not gone at all as he had planned. Whenever he passed by Peter's table, Norman made some kind of murmured remark against his father and his controlling ways. Peter decided it was better to ignore the comments, just let Norman express his displeasure. He was pretty certain he could make Norman feel better when they were alone together later. It was another two hours before Norman could get away and Peter was glad that he had been judicious in how much he had imbibed.

Norman was still scowling as he moved to join Peter.

"Come on, let us get out of here," Norman said.

"Easy, my friend," Peter said quietly as they walked away from the tavern. "Leave the foul temper behind. I know how to make you relax."

Norman smiled. "Aye, you do indeed. Hard to believe you were as innocent as a babe only a few months since."

They continued on to their private little place: a pile of sacking in the hay loft of the barn that lay half-way between Peter's home and the tavern. They disrobed quickly and Norman pushed Peter down so suddenly that he landed on the sacking with a grunt of surprise.

"Want you," Norman murmured, his hands sliding over Peter's chest.

Norman tweaked a nipple before continuing down to Peter's stomach. He looked into Peter's eyes and Peter saw the heat and desire in his lover's gaze. He smiled and said, "I want you too, Norman. You make me feel so alive."

Norman growled and took a hold of Peter's prick, squeezing the head before sliding his hand down to the base nestling in a mass of dark brown curls. Norman leaned down and pressed his face into Peter's pubic hair, inhaling his scent for a moment, before pulling back and licking the head of Peter's prick. Peter moaned and squirmed at the wonderful feeling. He loved it when Norman used his mouth on him, he loved the heat and the sensation of being completely consumed; it was almost as good as the sense of being swallowed by Norman when Peter thrust his cock deep into Norman's body. Yet that was not what he desired this time.

"Not that way tonight," Peter ground out. "I want you inside me. I want to feel you so deep that everything else fades away."

"Yes, yes," Norman agreed. "Let us leave all our problems behind."

Peter rolled over and got onto his hands and knees, while Norman fumbled through his clothes until he pulled out a small pot of salve. Peter knew he'd have brought it, Norman always came prepared. It did not take long for Norman to get him ready and Peter gasped when he felt Norman's prick press against his hole.

He strove to relax and let Norman breach him and they both sighed as Norman steadily pushed inside. Norman's weight was heavy on Peter's back and Peter could feel the thundering of Norman's heart. Even as Peter's body settled with the familiarity of Norman on him and in him, Norman pulled almost all the way out of his body and then thrust back in.

Peter grunted and then Norman was pounding into him with purpose. Peter cried out and threw back his head as Norman found that special spot deep inside. Norman growled and plunged deeper into Peter.

"God, more…keep doing…*Jesu*! Harder," Peter cried. He felt as if he was on fire and the heat was searing through his whole body. He wanted more; he wanted it never to end. It was glorious. Norman grasped Peter's prick, which was hard and leaking, and he slid his hand up and down to the rhythm of his thrusts into Peter's body. Peter was no longer capable of words, he could only feel and rejoice as he soared higher and higher.

"Ah, God," Norman groaned and spilled his seed into Peter who shuddered, cried out and shot his semen onto the sacking.

Norman laughed and tumbled to the side, bringing Peter with him to lie with his back against Norman's chest. "That was wondrous," Norman said.

"Aye, best ever." Peter smiled and rolled into Norman's embrace, leaned in to take a kiss. Norman groaned and opened his mouth. Kissing wasn't something they did as often as Peter liked but, though Norman rarely initiated it, he never failed to lose himself in the joining. They separated and Peter settled against Norman, enjoying just lying in his arms.

Peter knew he and Norman could never be more than this, more than a few hours stolen in the darkness, but it would have to be enough. He had never spoken of love to Norman for he didn't know how his friend—his lover—would react to such words, but Peter had come to believe that what he felt for Norman was the nearest to love he would ever feel.

He also realized something else, that it was past time he accepted the reality of his life. He had to stop fighting his mother and shoulder the responsibility of taking over control of the family farms. He would have to take a wife one day, but he knew he would never love a woman. He could only hope he would at least like the woman he would have to spend his life with. He looked at Norman and sadness stole over him.

"It is almost dawn, Peter." Norman yawned but pushed himself up and away from Peter. "I need to get back in my room before it is too late."

"Yes, me too. Norman?"

"Hmm," Norman asked, grabbing his clothes. He glanced at Peter. "What?"

"I…" Peter stopped, chewing his lip. Was he being a fool to even think of asking?

"Come on, Peter, out with it."

"Me, you, is it just to get…Just for a tumble in the hay?"

Norman smiled. "In the beginning, perhaps. But now, it is more." He shrugged. "Do not know what exactly, but when I'm with you I feel something." Surprisingly, Norman's face flushed.

Peter stepped toe to toe with Norman, slipping his arms around his neck. "Good. You mean *something* to me, too. Something special, Norman. I am not expecting you to feel the same, but I want you to know. I love you."

A gasp escaped Norman and he pulled Peter closer. "Thank God, I have been in love with you for what seems like forever."

Peter tightened his embrace and this time it was Norman who swooped in and kissed him.

▲

About Stevie Woods

STEVIE WOODS HAS been writing gay erotic romance for several years now after stumbling over the genre and being immediately smitten. She has a soft spot for historical, but also likes to try other genres, finding the similarities as intriguing as the differences.

She has novels and novellas published in both eBook and Print by Amber Quill Press, MLR Press, Torquere Press and Phaze Books. You can find out about her various works, one-off stories and series, on her website together with the necessary links.

Website: steviewoods.com
Blog: swquill.wordpress.com
Livejournal: swquill.livejournal.com
Facebook: facebook.com/profile.php?id=100001969101724
Twitter: @StevieWoods
Goodreads: goodreads.com/author/show/1200331.Stevie_Woods
GLBT Wiki: bookworld.editme.com/StevieWoods
Email: stevie@steviewoods.com

The Utterly True History of Guy Alien and the Rise and Fall of His Band, X-Wing
by Stevie Carroll

JONATHAN BANKS CAME to Oxford in 1986, because the Polytechnic had offered him a place (on a course he lasted on for all of one term and three weeks). He stayed in Oxford, because signing on there and living in a crappy rented flat was better than signing on at home and living with his parents. He started a band with thoughts of Lucas' B-movie revival, and Bowie's Space Oddity phase at the forefront of his mind. Hence the names he picked for both the band, and for his stage persona.

At the auditions—he held proper auditions, rather than taking on the first musicians to reply to his ad in the corner shop—Guy's check-list was based less on musical ability and more on the look of his band. He also considered how long they could stay together without killing each other: a break-up due to 'musical differences' wasn't in his plans.

He needed band members who could play, that went without saying, but he didn't want anyone who could play too much better than he could. This was Guy's band, and the rest of them were supposed to make him look good. Guy didn't want anyone leaving the band behind at a later date because of a better offer:

especially not one based on their talent.

The prospective band members he clicked with—and ended up living with—all wanted to play hard rock: discordant riffs, and lyrics about lost love. In the end, after many heated debates over multiple bottles of Jack Daniels, they kept the name for the band, if not the image Guy had envisioned. Their eyeliner was smudged (no other make-up barring a trace of lip-gloss if the beer and sweat hadn't washed it away), and their jeans were strategically ripped, but there was still enough glamour in X-Wing for Guy Alien.

Guy bleached his hair—it was easier than waiting for the dye to wash out—and let the sister of one of his new bandmates cut it to match the others. He bought jeans in Oxfam then ripped them in all the appropriate places, and threw out his latex and sequins. After a few rehearsals, he almost liked this new look.

⨭

"WHAT'S THAT YOU'RE reading?"

"Something I picked up at the record fair. It's from two years ago, but there's a retrospective-cum-promotional piece on someone you used to know."

"Let's see...*Queer Chord*—I remember that zine—I wrote reviews for it a couple of times."

"Did you write this piece?"

"Don't think I wrote anything for that issue. What's it say anyway? Budge up a bit, and I'll read over your shoulder."

⨭

THEY LAUNCHED INTO gigging after only a month or two of rehearsals. One of the guys had a friend whose sister needed a band for her party, having been let down at short notice. They played covers, mostly, which went down pretty well, and a couple of their own songs (hastily penned by Guy the night the gig was confirmed), which weren't a complete disaster.

That gig led to others, and then to a regular slot at the Jericho Tavern. They didn't get paid much, but the beer—if not the whiskey—was free. Guy penned more songs, using riffs and snatches of lyrics written by one or more of the other band members—but only if they made his parts look good. X-Wing would always be Guy's band, no matter who else played in it. He was the brains behind it, the front man—lead singer and lead guitarist—and the one who drove the publicity. Guy was the one who got first pick of the groupies. Slowly but surely, the band were acquiring those as well.

⋏

"THAT'S NOT QUITE how I remember it."

"Really?"

"Guy didn't write all the songs for one thing."

"And the groupies?"

"Were talked about more than seen—at least when I was hanging out with the band."

⋏

AT SCHOOL GUY (known as Jonathan back then) had looked at boys a little too closely to consider himself completely straight, but before James—the skinny kid with the pointed features, the over-long fringe and the huge dark eyes—all of Guy's groupies had been female. The other guys didn't much mind James, so long as Guy kept up the pretence that one backstage (back room, broom cupboard, far end of the gents) blow-job was the same as another. It wasn't—not really—because James was better than any girl Guy had ever had. James was also a walking music encyclopaedia, which would have put him a step above the other groupies in the band's eyes, had he not been American and male.

"THEY DIDN'T LIKE you being American? Why ever not?"

"Half the band thought Richards and Jagger were far superior to any of their US influences, and the other half wanted to resurrect the New Wave of British Heavy Metal. So, no, I wasn't exactly popular with them."

"So could it have been one of them that wrote the article? All these details about Guy's sex life seem very explicit for a promo piece."

"It's *Queer Chord*: they always liked to have a bitchy angle. The more explicitly about sex the better, from what I remember. Guy wouldn't have liked it, but what could he have done? Complaining after publication would have just got that part of the article picked up by a proper music paper."

"It doesn't bother you? Being written about like that?"

"It all happened years ago. I'm hardly likely to lose work over it now, am I? I don't see you storming off in a huff either."

▲

GUY NEVER WENT down on James. Half the time he didn't even bother to wank him off, and never when there were other band members around. More than half the time Guy was convinced that James was thinking of someone else. The rest of the time James was seriously enthusiastic about kissing (as serious and enthusiastic as he was about music). Guy wondered what James wasn't telling him, and where his boyfriend went when not at uni—James belonged to a proper Oxford college—or hanging around the band.

Annoyingly, James was better at finding new contacts for the band than Guy had ever been. He'd written gig and demo reviews for the student press and underground zines— photocopied in college libraries and held together with 'borrowed' staples—before he met Guy. James took photographs, at gigs and around town, 'donating' some to the same indie publications that printed his reviews, and selling others to bigger outfits. It was James that landed X-Wing their first hours of studio time, got their demo cassettes recorded on the cheap, and produced the illustrations and lettering for their demos' sleeves. The band moved closer to stardom in those five weeks than it had in the previous two years.

It became obvious that James would have to go before the band hit the big time, which meant that he had to go soon. He was bound to want a cut of any real money they eventually made, and what rock band's front man had an ever-present boyfriend? Even Bowie was straight these days. James sent their second demo tape to John Peel after it had been played a few times on local radio shows late at night, and the band let him stay—at least until the end of term. The tape never got played, and the band started hassling Guy—more seriously this time—to ditch James.

▲

"ARE YOU SURE you didn't write this piece? It's giving you a lot of credit for what happened in the space of—what was it? Six weeks? Five?"

"More like seven. Not my writing, but I'd love to know whose it was. He seems to know a lot about me."

"I never knew you had contacts at any recording studios."

"I didn't. That was Chrissie. She was shagging the drummer before I knew any of them, but he dumped her for shagging one of the guys at the studio behind his back."

▲

JAMES WENT BACK to America for Christmas, and Guy found a regular girlfriend. She gave him back the credibility that James had lost him, and came to all the band's gigs and rehearsals, just as James had. She knew nearly as much about obscure bands as James, although Guy never heard her play the guitar that lived below her largest Steve Vai poster (James had fancied Steve Vai as well).

Guy almost dumped James long-distance, though not as long-distance as he'd hoped for, when James called from a phone box in London to say he'd flown back early. Could they meet up? Guy wasn't totally heartless, and came up with plausible excuses why James couldn't stay at his place until term started. James seemed unperturbed: there was a guy he knew, and a squat he could stay in, somewhere in London—and hey, weren't X-Wing playing Camden Underworld next week anyway?

When James showed up at the London gig, Guy snogged him for old times' sake before telling him they were over. The girlfriend dumped Guy the next morning, taking off with Guy's best guitar, the red and black Fender Stratocaster, along with his money from the gig, and his train ticket back to Oxford.

▲

"THAT'S NOT QUITE how it was either."

"You surprise me."

"Frankie *lent* Guy the Strat. It was never his, but he acted like it was."

"Now why doesn't that surprise me?"

▲

BY EASTER THE band was a man down and they'd lost their regular slot at the Jericho Tavern. To make matters worse, James was about to shack up with one of the not-completely-ancient Dons that he drank with now he didn't drink with the band. Different college, different faculty, he said, like that made all the difference to the student-lecturer dodginess of it all. The bloke was good looking, in an older, intellectual, been-around-a-bit, kind of way, and he played acoustic guitar. James said he played it better than Guy played his electric, which smarted more than anything else might have. The Don came from money. James liked money, even though he seemed to have plenty of his own.

▲

"I PLAY BETTER than Guy, do I?"
"Isn't that what I've always told you?"
"Perhaps. And if you like money so much, why do all your clothes seem to come from Oxfam?"
"Because I'm an individual?"
"You're certainly that."

▲

THE BAND PICKED up a few gigs over the summer, although no one wanted to hear their new songs. Guy found himself a job—at the Jobcentre, of all places—and so did the others, though those were mostly shelf-stacking. They moved out of their squat into rented flats in different parts of town, and everyone but Guy found a steady girlfriend.

▲

"NO GIRLFRIEND FOR poor old Guy, then?"
"You never liked him."
"Can you blame me? I hope it was me you were thinking of all those times you were snogging him."
"You or Steve Vai."

▲

THEIR DRUMMER WAS the first to get married. The gig at his

reception was also his farewell. Guy never managed to find a permanent replacement, but there was always someone prepared to wield the sticks if and when X-Wing got a gig. Not that there were many gigs to be had, as the eighties slowly slid towards the nineties.

Guy thought about leaving Oxford. He applied for a transfer when their bass player left to help his girlfriend with their new baby, and again when X-Wing's original keyboard player somehow got a job in the City. Guy barely understood his own finances, much less how anyone he knew was capable of handling other people's. Both of those times, his application was passed over, in much the same way as his opportunities for promotion. After the second knock-back Guy thought about cutting his hair, but there was always a chance the band might make it one day. He needed to have the right look if they were going to be successful.

▲

"VERY *SPINAL TAP*, that drummer problem."

"Nah, just Guy treating them like dirt. He never had any respect for the rhythm section."

▲

A YEAR LATER, bisexual rock stars were back in fashion. The two other band members that had lasted the distance, though now with shorter hair and long fringes like James had had, began to ask whatever had happened to that boyfriend Guy had briefly had. Their old musical style had fallen out of favour, and this latest trend wouldn't fit them without a more drastic image shift.

Guy scoured the music press, bought all the zines he could lay his hands on, listened to every demo he saw advertised on fliers in pubs and clubs. None of the new bands appealed to him in the way that his old dreams had, not that his old dreams had ever come to much. He searched around for anyone from the old crowd that still had their finger on the pulse of the music industry.

He found James.

⚲

"WHEN WAS THAT? I don't remember him coming here."

"He didn't. You were off on a dig somewhere, and I'd stayed behind to have my essay crisis in peace. No way was I going to let him see just how big a place your money bought us."

⚲

JAMES MET GUY for a pint and told him how well his degree and his relationship had been working out for him in the two years since their last meeting. He was hoping to become a photojournalist when he graduated: James was studying PPE, but didn't want to go into politics. He talked of travelling the world in search of stories, then coming home to that Don he'd fallen for back when he arrived in Oxford.

Guy was a little disappointed to find he hadn't been James' first love, or even his first love after music. He was more disappointed that James was lining up overseas trips (in his head at least) that left far behind any touring Guy had ever planned to do with X-Wing.

Guy outlined all that had happened with X-Wing—his career. The Jobcentre wasn't a career; it just paid his rent and kept him in beer and food. He blamed the band's decline firmly on his ex and her theft of his lucky guitar, and maybe a little on James for accepting being dumped so easily. Not that he'd told James the last part, of course.

James sympathised over the loss of the guitar—he of all people understood how that rankled more than any break-up— before pointing out that Guy's ex-girlfriend and her current band had done a live session for John Peel just last week. Guy wondered whether he should look her up next—see if she needed a roadie or anything.

Luckily for Guy, James knew exactly how to get hold of her. They sometimes played the Jericho Tavern, but mostly they had paying gigs at bigger venues. There was one coming up in less than a week.

▲

"SO MUCH FOR your essay crisis."

"I can do more than one thing at once, when I want to."

"You can show me later, if you like."

▲

IT WAS AS well that he went to Frankie's band's next gig. Guy's ex had broken up with Natasha, her rhythm guitarist, only the week before, and urgently needed a permanent replacement: in the band, if not in her bed. Was Guy interested?

Guy almost turned her down—he wasn't going to forgive her for taking his guitar—but then he saw Andy, her band's bass player. There might have been a return spark of interest as well, but then Guy had always had a healthy imagination and an over-large ego.

Who knew? This band might even get him into the charts at least one time, before fashions changed again.

▲

"AND DID THEY? Make the charts, I mean."

"Not while Guy was playing guitar for them. The band had a number one in the indie charts after they threw him out."

"You almost make me feel sorry for him..."

"Oh, Guy always bounced back. Last thing I heard he was

working in a guitar shop in Bicester, and playing covers at the Wendlebury Arms on Thursday nights. Apparently he's straight again too, just like Bowie. Bloody wannabe-bisexuals."

"I thought we agreed you weren't going to say anything against bisexuals."

"Not you. You're a proper bisexual."

"Glad you think so. Don't think we need to read any more of that rag right now, do we?"

"Got a better suggestion?"

"It's a Saturday, I don't have any essays to mark, and you're back home from 'travelling the world' as the article put it, for the first time in a month. Of course I've got a better suggestion."

"We going upstairs then?"

"I suppose we should. Unless you *want* to put on a show for anyone who happens to be passing along the road."

"I'm respectable these days, aren't I?"

"I'll believe that when I see it."

▲

About Stevie Carroll

BORN IN SHEFFIELD: England's Steel City, and raised in a village on the boundary of the White and Dark Peaks, Stevie Carroll was nourished by a diet of drama and science fiction from the BBC and ITV, and a diverse range of books, most notably Diane Wynne-Jones and The Women's Press, from the only library in the valley. After this came a university education in Scotland, while writing mostly non-fiction for various underground bisexual publications under various aliases, before creativity was stifled by a decade of day-jobs.

Now based in Hampshire, Stevie has rediscovered the joys of writing fiction, managing to combine thoughts of science fiction, fantasy and mysteries with a day-job in the pharmaceuticals industry and far too many voluntary posts working with young people, with animals and in local politics. Stevie's first published story, "The Monitors" (in Noble Romance's *Echoes of Possibilities*), was long listed by the 2010 Tiptree Awards jury.

Stevie currently has multiple projects on the boil, including at least two novels, a novella and several short stories. Updates on all of these are currently to be found at Stevie's Livejournal, although a website is in the planning stages and will go live towards the end of the year if not before.

Livejournal: stevie-carroll.livejournal.com
Email: stevie.carroll@dormouse.myzen.co.uk

Fantasy Man
by Jay Rookwood

AND THEN I'M flat on my back, his full weight crushing me like an avalanche. He has me at his mercy, his conquered slave, his toy, and the exhilaration and terror of it twists and coils like a hagfish in my belly. I wonder how big his cock might be as his free hand pops the buttons of his fly. "I'm gonna fuck you good," Alex grunts as he stuffs a lube-slicked finger deep inside me, "fuck you and make you beg for more."

My arse-guts slacken almost as if salivating, gasping to be filled by him. I pull my legs out to the sides, leaving the way open.

"Eager, eh? Want me now? You want me to plough you hard and deep?" The helmet of his invading army is battering at the gates. "Are you sure you're ready for this much?" He grins as he pulls back like an archer pulling on an arrow, his body tense as he prepares to drive into me. My blood surges with a mix of need and terror.

He wraps his massive arms around me and holds me in tightly, controlled, dominated, then surges up and forwards. The head of his dick pushes past my hungry sphincter and I gasp as he fills me, fulfils me, gulping for air like a drowning perch. "You think this feels good? Just wait till you've got the other seven inch..."

"Mack, the kitch...oh!" And the fantasy pops like an over-inflated balloon. Back to life, back to reality. Back to the here and now.

"Yeah? Julie, you *know* to knock before you come in my room." Julie's my kid sister. She's seven and has a mass of blonde frizz which proudly proclaims a mixed-race heritage that in me is hidden by pale flesh and skinhead. I've been looking after her on my own ever since Dad died almost five years ago, just months after I finished my GCSEs.

"Sorry, Mack." The door closes and I'm left to myself again, but Julie has successfully killed the mood. I'd been close, too. I jump out of bed, towel off the sweat, pull my jogging bottoms up and my T-shirt down, making myself at least vaguely presentable. I'm far from suitable to be seen in public, but at least I'm no longer *in flagrante delicto*.

I pad down the passage and up into the big open-plan room at the front, then double back into the kitchen where Julie is yanking on the tap. Our flat is the top half of a Victorian semi not far from the centre of Torquay, and has all the advantages and disadvantages that go with older buildings—nice and cool in summer, but icy in winter and continual plumbing problems.

"It's stuck again, Mack."

I give the handle a tug, but it refuses to move. I tug harder, then harder again until there's a dull crack and water hisses out of the base of the handle, quickly trickling down through the gap where the tap doesn't quite fit snugly to the sink. "Damn, and it's Friday night too—I hope I can get a plumber before Monday." I duck under the sink to flip the isolation valve, but it refuses to move. The water is already dripping steadily down the pipes, and directly below are the Victorian floorboards. Water is probably already pooling on the ceiling of the flat beneath.

With no other way to stop the water, I shift sideways and turn off the stop-cock. The dripping gradually slows then stops altogether. I look at Julie, "The only way to stop the water was to turn off the water for the whole flat, so we now have no water at all. I'll have to take you over to Geri's and see if her mum won't mind bathing you this evening, and perhaps let you sleep over. Then hopefully I'll be able to find a plumber who'll come out tomorrow." I look at the rickety old pine table in the dining room, already nearing the limits of what my meagre DIY skills can fix; there's no way I'll get a replacement now. We'll just have to go without for a while.

▲

I RETURN FROM dropping Julie off at her best friend Geri's house on the other side of Torquay, and see my new downstairs neighbour Vic coming out of her front door; it's only then that I remember her husband works as a kitchen fitter.

If you're straight, Victoria Yorke is all kinds of hot made manifest: petite and boyishly cute with short-cropped cherry-blonde hair and dimples. If it weren't for the swell of her belly and breasts you'd think from the way she dresses Vic was a hot male university student; she could easily get me feeling very confused if I was into younger lads.

"Heya, Vic. How are *we* this evening?"

"Hey, Mack, *we* are doing just fine. All four of us."

"Four?"

"I'm carrying triplets, the hospital confirmed it by ultrasound a few hours ago." There's something off about the tone of her voice, as if there's a bad side to this as well, but I give a congratulatory hug anyway. "I'm just off to work so I can't stop and chat."

"Sure. Is Al in?"

"Got back a few minutes ago. What do you need my big strong man for? Something too heavy for you to lift?" She grins. I've never hidden that I'm gay—it wasn't ever really an option, seeing as how a mutual acquaintance had already outed me to Vic and Alex before I ever met them. It doesn't seem to make any difference to how Alex and Vic treat me but, despite the banter, I don't feel entirely comfortable with them knowing. I'm constantly worried the bodice-ripper fantasies on the inside could show through the innuendo on the outside.

"Hahaha no, no lifting required. Well, except possibly his tool box—I've got a leak in the kitchen."

She rolls her eyes at my weak humour. "That he should be able to help you with. He's in the bedroom getting changed out of his work gear." She calls back over her shoulder, "It's Mack, he's got a problem with his pipes." She turns back to me, "I'll see you boys later."

"Come straight in Mack." I follow Alex's voice through to the bedroom; he's half dressed, wearing old running bottoms which, judging by how closely they hug his thighs, were bought when he was far less massive.

Did I mention that Alex is a body-builder? And I don't mean one of your little gym queens either; the phrase "built like a house" would only apply to him if you included the Tower of London in your definition of "house". He's 6'5" and, at over twenty-one stone, about three times his wife's weight and almost twice mine. Conversations with Vic invariably revolve around either her pregnancy or Alex's upcoming début on the professional competition circuit.

"So what can I do for you?"

"My kitchen tap's broken, and I'm no good at plumbing. I wondered if you might give me a hand?"

He gives an easy smile, and the room spins briefly. "Give me five minutes to get back into my work gear and we can go get my tools out of the van."

"Wow, your tools are really so big that even you need a second person to handle them, eh?"

Alex rolls his eyes in perfect mimicry of Vic a few seconds earlier.

The fix isn't complicated, but Alex decides to replace the taps rather than fix them. "Fortunately for you I have some taps from a job I did today. They can't be more than a year old, and they're way better than these old things. I'd only throw them away otherwise." He squeezes into the cupboard to unscrew the old taps, and I take the opportunity to stare at his body. I don't feel comfortable ogling him openly, normally, but for once he can't see me. His loose T-shirt rides up his body as he reaches up behind the sink, and I feast my eyes on the broad torso. It's the off-season so Alex has been packing on weight. The extra meat looks good on his already-overpowered frame.

"Mack, the hot tap's loose so I'm having problems unscrewing it. Can you grab it and hold it in place?"

I step over him, one leg either side of his chest, and grab the tap, holding on tightly as it shakes and tries to pull from my grip. I feel myself lengthening at having all that muscle so close beneath me, and for once curse being so well-hung; there's no way I can hide my exhilaration, and I pray Alex doesn't notice.

"Okay, now the cold tap." This tap is much stiffer, and I find my leg pressed against Alex's side as I brace myself to keep it from turning. My balls twitch traitorously, and the tap almost slips in my hands. I close my eyes; try to ignore the firm heat against my calf.

"Right, that's it. You can pull them both out and put the new taps in."

Twenty minutes later I have two replacement taps, a new isolation valve and quite a lot of mess on the floor. I put my hand down to help Alex back to his feet. "What do I owe you?"

"Oh, don't worry about that."

"You've done over an hour's work and given me two taps, a new valve and about four foot of copper pipe. I really should pay you. I owe you."

He tests the taps then cleans off his hands under the hot water. "The taps were effectively free and those valves are only a couple of quid, plus all that water could have ruined my bedroom. But if you do feel you should give me something, there is a favour you could do me."

"Sure, what needs doing?"

"I could really do with a blowjob."

For a moment I wonder if I need my ears checked. "You what?"

"I could do with a blowjob."

So I wasn't hallucinating. "Okay, um, what the fuck? Is this some kind of sick joke? What about Vic?"

"She's fine with it, we have an open relationship. Plus I've barely even seen her since we moved in. I get back just as she's off to work, and most weekends either I'm not here or she isn't. And she's kinda gone off sex. She doesn't much like being pregnant."

I cock an eyebrow at him. "You really are serious? Al, I appreciate being asked, and I'm not saying I don't want to give you one—believe me, I'd love to, you're not the only one in the middle of a dry spell here. But I don't feel right with you cheating on Vic with me."

"It's only cheating if you're in a closed relationship."

"It still don't feel right."

He shrugs and goes to pick up his tool box, then stops and just looks at me. "I really can't convince you?"

"I wish you could, but it just don't feel right."

"Perhaps a kiss would do it?"

"No, Alex, I don't—" but the moment his lips hit mine, my brain outsources all cognitive functions to my dick. He starts off gentle, but pretty soon I've let him press himself against me, all hard heat and muscle pushing me against the wall.

"Convinced?"

I nod mutely as he smiles down at me, almost too gentle for a man his size. What little hope of resistance I have left is wiped out seeing such a smile on that square, handsome face.

I drop to my knees and slide my hand up the back of his thigh, inside his work shorts, stroking the thick muscles there as I press my face into his crotch. He begins to pull his zip down, but I stop him; it's a while since I've last done this for another man, and I intend to take my time, to savour the experience. I move down to nuzzle at the head of his dick, feeling it swell underneath the tough, paint-spattered cotton. It's more impressive than I'd expected—as long as my own, though not as thick;

the rest of him is so big it makes his dick seem far more average than it is unless you're this close in.

I glance up to see Alex's eyes urge me on, and my hand moves higher in his shorts to feel the base of his granite-hard arse pulse under my hand as the muscles tighten and quiver at my touch. I slide a finger into the slick, slippery crack, feel his cherry pulsate against my fingertip as Alex lets out a whimper. I relent, opening his fly. He's freeballing, and I push my face into his unshaven crotch again, my balls smouldering as the stench of his fresh mansweat fills my nose. "Go for it, please." Alex's voice is hoarse, barely a whisper.

I pull his shorts down slowly, sucking at the topside of his shaft as it's exposed. His cut shaft is lean and swells slightly at the middle, and behind it balls the size of hen's eggs hang loose and low. He's already drooling salt-sweet precome. My need finally gets the better of self-control and I deep-throat almost the entire length in one move.

"Fuuuuck." Alex's legs lose their strength and he leans heavily back on the counter behind him. His dick almost comes out of my mouth, and I react by plunging forward, gulping him down. The sensation of having him thrust so far past my tonsils is incredible—for the first time I understand why so many guys love deep-throating my own larger dick. I look up at Alex's face, and there's a definite look of shock-and-awe.

"A little…slower…maybe?" But this isn't me doing him a favour any more—it's me needing him in a way I'm still not ready to admit even to myself. I pull back then inhale his shaft once more, then again, and again, feeling his balls pulling up towards the base of his dick. Then his thighs tense and his dick jerks inside me as the pulse of his hot come shoots down my throat. With him thrust in so deeply, I have no choice but to swallow his load.

Alex gives a slight groan, and slides down to the floor, taking me with him. It's taken barely a few minutes and, while Alex is sated, all I've achieved for myself is to stoke my own desire.

Any pretence at virtue and modesty is long gone, and I slake my thirst for him, his muscles, his power. He lays there a while, but whether in tolerance or enjoyment I neither know nor care.

Then one large, strong hand clamps itself to my butt and I find myself being pulled away as its counterpart pushes into my jogging bottoms, grasping for my dick and balls. He pulls on them hard and my body responds, my most secret fantasies flooding through my mind and through my flesh as I yield to him, wanting him to use my body in whatever way he wishes.

But by this point I'm already so close that it takes just seconds to bring me off. My body stiffens as I detonate like a Tsar-bomba, my come machine-gunning into Alex's rough hand, the wind crushed out of my lungs. But I barely have time to notice this as my legs spasm and stiffen, my brain scrambling for control before the agony of a pulled muscle screams up from my left calf.

When my body finally relaxes enough to let me breathe I let out a gasping yelp, and Alex pulls me in closely, lovingly, clearly not realising the pain I'm in—or the emotional turmoil. My brain's outsourcing contract has been revoked, and already my belly is churning with revulsion and anger at what we've done.

I feel the tears on my cheeks before I even realise I'm crying.

"Get out." I feel him shift beneath me, and I look up into a face of surprise and pain, but my fury is fed by the persistent throb of my calf and I push on regardless. "I said get out. Now."

"Mack, what's wrong?"

"What's wrong? What's…fucking…wrong?" I shift away from him, and the pain in my calf blooms too quickly for me to hide it from him. He backs away, my weight shifts again and my leg screams blue murder yet again. "I just want to be left alone."

"I'm sorry if you're annoyed…"

"You think I'm merely annoyed? Right now I want to rip your bollocks off, Alex. I said we shouldn't do this, and you went ahead anyway. Now *get out*."

"Let me at least get you to a sofa, get you some pain-killers."

"I don't want your help, Al, and if you so much as move to

touch me, I will…" But I realise the threat is hollow even as I make it. There's nothing I can do to him. I turn my face away and let the tears flow; it's some time later before I look back. He's already gone.

The hollow feeling in my chest widens until I'm looking out across the Valles Marineris, and all I want is to be held in his arms, for him to be totally mine. But deep down I know that this caring, gentle, protective Alex is as about as real as the one who stalks my fantasies, ripping my clothes off and taking me for his plaything.

I cannot stop crying.

⋏

THE DOORBELL RINGS about half past eleven, and I peer into the greyscale intercom screen. It's Vic, still in her work clothes. "Can I come up?"

I still feel sick and stained from what I did with Alex earlier, my eyes are sore and dry, and the pain in my lower leg, which I have to hold doubled-back against my thigh to keep from screaming, is preventing sleep. "I'm really tired, Vic."

"I won't keep you long, I just…I need to talk to you about what happened earlier."

No beating around the bush then. "Look, I'm really sorry, Vic. It—"

"Please let me up, Mack."

I give in and hit the key button on the intercom, then hear her coming up the stairs as I hop over to the couch. It takes some time to carefully get myself into the least painful position I can find. "I've pulled a muscle in my leg," I explain as Vic appears, just as I am getting settled.

"How did you…it wasn't while you were with Alex, was it?"

"With?"

"You know what I mean." She sits down on the rug cross-legged, and the way her T-shirt falls accentuates her swelling belly, reminding me of precisely what I've done.

"So he told you. Look, I'm sorry, Vic. It wasn't like I intended—"

"You don't need to apologise to me, Mack. Not when it's partly my fault for getting the two of you into this situation in the first place."

"What?" My brain, still fuzzy with insomnia, is barely in the same book let alone on the same page. "Your fault since when?" Cogs begin to turn. "It's not your fault you're not feeling like sex right now, I imagine it's not unusual under the circumstances. But Alex could at least try to keep his dick in his own pants!"

She smiles maternally, and somehow I know I'm being blind, but I can't yet understand why. The putrid feeling starts to abate, but only because it's being pushed aside by an equally unsettled confusion. "Mack, I am the one who needs to apologise to you. It was my idea. Alex won't see it like that, he'll say it was his decision so his fault, but ultimately it was my fault that you two did…whatever it was you did. I thought…no, that's the problem, I didn't think. I just assumed. I assumed you wanted it, assumed he'd be sensitive, assumed…I don't know, assumed it would all work."

"This isn't making sense."

"I'm afraid I'm not very good at the Machiavelli routine." She moves to sit at the other end of the sofa, holding her limbs in uncomfortably tight, looking at the floor. "A few weeks ago I gave Alex permission to go find a short-term…mistress sounds too formal a word, but you get the idea. I've never been the jealous type. We've always had an open relationship, but we normally play together so this is new territory for both of us. I just hate seeing him so frustrated. But he wasn't comfortable with having sex with someone he might get attached to. We had this big argument, and I said that maybe he should find a gay man to fuck." She puts her face in her hands. "God! I even mentioned you by name."

The sick feeling that had been slowly curdling away in my belly evaporates, burned away by fury. "You think that makes it okay? You think pushing him onto me is fine, because *he* won't get attached? What about me, what if I get attached? What if I don't want to give him up?"

"Mack, I'm so sorry, I should never have done it. It was stupid, so, so stupid. I don't know exactly what went wrong between you, but I really wish I'd never said anything."

"I sucked off someone else's husband is what went wrong, Vic. I sucked him off and it was incredible, and no matter how sick and filthy I feel because of it, no matter how guilty for playing the home-wrecker, it doesn't stop how much I want him. A few hours ago it was just a fantasy, but now it's been made real and it's something I can't have because he's yours, and now I find that you are the one who told him to do this? Sorry, Vic, but apology not accepted."

She turns to face me, tries to take my hand in hers but I pull away. "You're not playing the home-wrecker, Mack. Really you aren't. I don't have a problem with you sleeping together. I wouldn't have suggested it otherwise."

I want to believe what I desire so desperately isn't wrong. I want to see it the way she does, and the idea of being his bit on the side, his willing come-bucket, does turn me on a lot. But he's not his own man: he has a wife and three kids on the way, and I can't believe it's right for me to let my fantasies intrude on their reality. "Perhaps we should just let this all cool down for a bit. Maybe after a few days we'll be able to see some way out of this mess."

She nods, relief flooding through her smile. "I really am very sorry, Mack. Please believe that." Then she gets up and is gone, and I'm left alone with my pain.

The one dimly-flickering spark of hope I have, that a straight man like Alex could ever feel anything for someone like me, seems a non-starter: Alex is hers. Even if he was interested in something more serious, I could never allow myself to break up a young family. It doesn't matter that she's happy for him to play around with me: I don't think I can reciprocate, I don't think I can share him.

But perhaps that's why there's still that little guttering vestige of hope: as long as I am unable to share, the only thing really standing between me and what I want is me.

▲

About Jay Rookwood

JAY ROOKWOOD REALISED he was genderqueer at twenty-five, after years of confusion over having two libidos—gay male and bisexual female. He's been writing for his own pleasure for years, but only recently started thinking about writing professionally. He hates most flying insects, and likes cats, dogs and spiders. Especially spiders.

On the Pull
by Elin Gregory

TOM WORKED FAST, shivering as the chill of the stone walls bit through the thin cotton of his shirt. He brushed his fringe out of his eyes with the back of his wrist and stooped again.

"What are you doing down there?" his mother called. "Tom?"

"Give me a minute!" Tom replied. "You can't rush perfection!"

As expected there was a roar of derision from above. Tom laughed as he raised the half pint glass high and peered at the treacle brown ale within. "Perfect," he breathed and hurried to connect the beer line. Job done, he stepped back to admire the rack of barrels. There were bigger, more modern pubs locally. But none of them took as much pride in the quality of their beer as The White Horse. There you got a decent pint in a straight glass poured the old fashioned way, cool to the lips but warming on its way down to settle comfortably in the belly. Most Saturday nights in summer were busy, but tonight The White Horse was entertaining Weston Stanage's village cricket team, and their well-beaten opponents, so the levels of beer had fallen fast. Luckily, Tom had planned ahead.

"Just so's you know—there's men dying of thirst up here." Mum peered down through the trapdoor at him. "Brian says he's coming over all faint. If you're done, I'm going to fetch more crisps."

Tom clambered up the ladder, slammed the trapdoor, and bowed in response to the cheer his customers gave when he popped back up behind the bar. "Right, that's a new barrel of Old Growler and one of Bishop's Finger," he said as he reached for a fresh glass.

"'Bout bloody time." Brian, Tom's team captain, put his empty glass on the bar. "Stop fannying about and pull me a pint." The rest of the team made encouraging noises, but fell silent as Tom approached the pump.

This was a ritual they all enjoyed. The first pint off a new barrel had to be pulled just right; there wasn't a man there who would rush him or complain about the delay. They would watch, their eyes fixed on the glass as the rich, dark brew trickled then gushed from the spigot, the creamy swirl separating as the head formed. Tom enjoyed putting on the show. He didn't think anyone there realised he had an agenda of his own.

Glass in his left hand, he wrapped the long fingers of his right around the satiny mahogany handle of the beer engine. He pulled, enjoying the resistance of it, knowing that the taut muscles of forearm and bicep were shown off by the motion.

Weston Stanage had not been a good place to come out. Everyone for miles around seemed to have an opinion to express. Some were bearable. Brian had been Tom's best mate since they could walk. He had laughed, said "No! You're kidding!" then said, "You don't fancy *me* do you?" adding, "Why not?" After that they had carried on as normal and most of Tom's friends, including the cricket team, had followed Brian's lead.

But there were always a few and the ones that smiled to your face but whispered behind your back were the worst. So, despite it being old news now, Tom was discreet about his courting. Not for him the admiring looks offered by the other bar staff; he was subtle about it and made the most of excellent peripheral vision. Tom knew his regulars, of course, and most of the visiting players from Sutton Stanage. They were up at the bar now, awaiting the first spurt of ale but there was just one whose attention had drifted from the beer to the beer provider.

Sutton's new player. Tom had faced him that afternoon along the rather tatty, sheep cropped pitch. He was nice looking, brown haired, medium sized, stocky and moved as though he was on springs. A good fielder, he had bowled competently, but it was his batting that shone. Thirty-five runs including a couple of impressive boundaries! Tom had admired him and speculated.

Then it was Tom's turn to bowl. Nothing fancy, just a nice slow ball with plenty of spin that veered around the offered bat to whip out the offside stump. "Howzat?" Tom had yelled, leaping into the air, shirt riding up over his belly. Sutton's new ace batsman had watched, giving Tom the kind of smile that shouldn't be allowed in public.

"Well, hello!" Tom had thought.

The batsman's name was Hugh, he was thirty-four, single, a doctor—Tom's mum got all the gossip. He was leaning on the bar a few paces away, talking to Sutton's captain, but his eyes were on Tom and that felt good. Tom adjusted his grip on the pump handle, thumb caressing the bright brass cap at the end of it. Oh, yes, that made Hugh's eyes widen a bit.

The beer line gurgled, the spigot spat, the glass began to fill.

"Oh, yeah," Brian murmured. Somebody else sighed.

Sometimes, when it was very quiet, Tom could hear the head forming on the pint, a soft comfortable hush, but tonight Tom's ears were pricked for something else. Glass brimming with deep chestnut brown, topped with creamy white, Tom raised it to let the light shine through.

"What do you think?" He asked, getting the usual answers, but it was Hugh's softly spoken "Looks pretty good to me," that he was listening for.

It took ten minutes to serve the crowd of players, supporters, wives and girlfriends. Tom handed two G&T's to Parker, the Sutton captain, exchanging polite, if insincere, smiles. Parker was a Daily Mail reader, and much inclined to repeating that rag's horror stories about declining standards and rising immorality.

However, since The White Horse had the best beer for miles, and Parker would never lower *his* standards, he still drank there, Tom notwithstanding.

Then it was Hugh's turn. He had contrived to be last in the queue and his smile as Tom said, "So—what can I do you for?" was bright.

"I'm a designated driver," he admitted.

"That's tragic. Your first trip to The White Horse, and you have to drink this muck?" Tom handed him an alcohol free lager. "I could weep."

"Well, there will definitely be other times," Hugh said. "Oh—Hugh May."

Tom shook his hand. It was a good handshake, firm without being overbearing, pleasantly unhurried.

"Tom Swan. Nice to meet you, Hugh. You're welcome any time."

Hugh grinned. "That's good to hear." His gaze skipped along the rank of beer pumps then back to Tom. "Looks like there's a lot to come back for."

They smiled at each other, but then Parker called. "May, a word in your ear, if you please?"

Hugh gave Tom an apologetic smile. "I'll see you later," he promised.

Tom watched him go—nice broad shoulders, that springy athletic walk, powered by what must surely be a superbly muscular arse—and chuckled as Hugh looked back, seeming pleased to catch him mid-ogle.

"Ahem!" An empty pint glass was waved under Tom's nose. "If you've got a minute..." Brian grinned at him as he leaned on the bar.

"Planning to get wazzed?" Tom asked, applying glass to spigot.

"That I am," Brian nodded. "Your sofa has my name on it because I want to celebrate stuffing stuck-up Sutton Stanage. I wanted to say that while I still can."

Some of the Sutton players did consider themselves a cut above. They all bought their whites at the same sporting outfitters, Weston wore what was clean. They had a pavilion, Weston put up a tent. But not all of them were as snootily objectionable as their captain.

"They're not all bad," Tom said.

"That new batsman of theirs, for instance," Brian began then stopped and grinned. "Oh, Tommy-boy, is that a blush I see? It is, isn't it? Well there's no point, because we already beat them. If you're planning to distract anyone, we're playing Whittle next week and they've got that fast bowler. Big Davy—you know the one. Works in the slaughterhouse. If anyone needs nobbling it's him."

"Wanker," Tom said and put the pint in his waiting hand. "No, I'm thinking ahead to next year."

"Good man. Maybe you can entice him over to our side?"

Tom chuckled, but his smile died when he looked across the room. Parker, lips thin, was hissing something to Hugh, who looked as though he wished he was somewhere, anywhere, else. Hugh glanced at Tom, confirming the subject of discussion then his gaze returned to his glass.

"Oh, shit," Brian groaned. "Nosy bloody Parker. He's such a—Tom, where you going?"

"I'm going to put the empty bottles out," Tom growled. The tub was only half full, but sometimes he just had to walk away. The whisperers, the sneerers, the bloody Parkers, made him wild—but it would be bad for business to punch out the captain of Sutton Stanage cricket team. And it would upset Mum.

Outside in the little back yard he separated the colours, tossing the bottles into the recycling bins with temper-relieving force as he tried to rationalise what had just happened. A doctor, Mum had said. In this day and age it shouldn't be anyone's business whether you liked girls, or blokes, or, for that matter, painting yourself with custard and hanging upside down in a cupboard, as long as everyone involved was happy with it. But some people made it their business, and for some professions the wrong sort of talk could make life horribly difficult.

Tom weighed a bottle in his hand as he heard a whoop and a round of applause from the pub. Man of the Match Award, he supposed. Probably Hugh—those two boundaries had been stunning. Tom dumped the bottle, feeling guilty. He should have stood his ground and been there to applaud.

The back door to the pub opened, and slammed shut. Tom looked round and stared. Hugh was striding towards him, his face white with fury.

"Nobody," Hugh snarled, "nobody has the right to tell me who I can be friends with. Nobody can dictate who I do or don't fancy. Right?"

"Er—right," Tom said, shocked but beginning to feel a little flutter of hilarious excitement. They stared at each other for a second more. Then Tom grabbed Hugh's shoulders, Hugh got a double handful of Tom's shirt, and their mouths met hard enough to make Tom's jaw twinge.

If he breaks it, at least he can set it, he thought. The only drawback—the only one—was that Hugh tasted slightly of that bloody awful alcohol-free lager. Otherwise—it was just brilliant.

They were breathing heavily when the kiss broke off.

"Whoa," Hugh murmured.

"Yeah," Tom agreed. They smiled into each other's eyes and Hugh grinned as Tom asked a question he had been mulling over. "Top or bottom?"

"Both—if that's okay with you?"

"Hell, yeah!"

Hugh chuckled. "Looks like you can pull more than just pints!"

Another kiss, more exploratory this time. Tom was pleased to note that the lager taste was less noticeable and that Hugh's hands on him felt very good indeed. Also, Hugh's arse was every bit as muscular as Tom had assumed. The yard may have smelled of dustbins, spilled beer and cats, but Hugh didn't seem to mind and neither did he. Just for the moment—as a starting point—it would do.

Light barred the paving as the back door opened again.

"What are you doing out there?" Mum called. "Tom?"

Hugh chuckled as Tom said, "Just give me a minute, Mum," and the next kiss was even sweeter. It lasted a long time, too—a very long time.

You can't rush perfection.

▲

About Elin Gregory

ELIN GREGORY HAS been writing stories for 50 years, initially in crayon, mostly for the fun of it, more recently to share with friends. She lives in Wales, is married and hopes, one day, to have a quiet little room of her own with lots of book shelving.

Frozen Angel
by Lisa Worrall

JOE PARKED THE car in the shade of an oak tree and turned off the engine. He glanced up at the cloudless, blue sky through his sun roof and smiled wistfully. It was the kind of summer day that you longed for when you were planning to spend it outside.

He climbed out of his old battered Renault and stretched, feeling his muscles complain and his back crack as his vertebrae realigned. The muscles across his shoulders were tense and sore with the effort of keeping his ancient car from pulling to the right on the two hour journey from his home in Essex to Finedon, Northamptonshire. Looking at the austere building in front of him, he smiled. Malc had been right, it was perfect, which was mildly surprising. He'd half expected to drive for two hours and then find himself standing in front of an old shed, but Malc had actually steered him in the right direction for once. St Mary the Virgin was a beautiful historic church on the road leading out of the sleepy village.

Joe pulled from his pocket the details he had printed off the net, and looked from the page to the church and then back again. St Mary's was a Grade 1 listed building that dated back to the fourteenth century, and the architecture was exquisite. He was going to be able to get some beautiful sketches here.

Leaning over the front seat, he grabbed his backpack and

sketch pad from behind the passenger seat and locked the car. He couldn't resist giving the hideous blue bonnet a congratulatory pat for having actually survived the journey, and getting them there in one piece. It may have been a problematic bucket of rust, but it was *his* problematic bucket of rust.

Joe walked along the path through the picturesque graveyard, weaving in and out of the headstones. His artist's eyes darted here and there, cataloguing the beautiful workmanship all around him. He felt the familiar frisson of excitement tingle up his spine, and his fingers itched to hold his pencil. When he made his way around the side of the church, Joe's breath caught in his throat. This was the one. He gazed at the angel before him.

Her eyes were closed, hands pressed together in prayer and her head slightly bent. He moved around her in a circle and marvelled at the slender arch of her neck, as smooth as silk with tendrils of hair curling at the nape. Whoever had sculpted this piece was a genius. The wings were a work of art in themselves. Each feather had been carefully crafted in minute detail to such an extent that Joe was sure if he touched them, he would feel the downy softness beneath his fingers. Angels were his forte. He had always been fascinated with them, even as a child, and when he discovered his talent for art, his fingers just naturally seemed to want to produce angels in all their beautiful forms.

Joe dropped his backpack onto the grass and slipped off his jacket, spreading it on the ground, before sitting down on it and toeing off his trainers. He picked up his sketch pad and rested it on his bent knees, curling his bare toes into the cool grass, sighing as the blades tickled his skin. The sun was warm on the back of his neck and he lifted his red-brown hair from his nape, feeling the slight summer breeze waft against his flesh. Then he picked up his pencil and put it to the paper.

He had no idea how long he had been sketching when a shadow fell across his pad and a deep voice said: "Wow." Looking up, Joe's breath hitched in his throat for the second time that morning. The blue eyes that met his were the same colour as the sky above him. Blue eyes that were surrounded by long pale lashes in a face so breathtakingly beautiful that, for a moment, he wasn't sure if he'd been sitting in the sun for too long and was hallucinating.

"Um…thanks," he said staring like a complete knob, when the vision shook his shoulder length blond hair and smiled brightly, revealing slightly crooked white teeth. Not that the slight imperfection made him any less of a vision. In Joe's opinion they only amped up this man's undeniable hotness.

"I'm sorry, I didn't mean to make you jump," the man said, holding his hand out palm up in a placating gesture. "I've been watching you for about half an hour. You were miles away." At the widening of Joe's green eyes, he shook his head quickly. "Shit! No, no, I didn't mean it in a stalkery, axe murdery kind of way. I just like to watch—oh, bollocks," he huffed out a laugh when Joe's lips twitched. "I'm not doing a very good job of convincing you I'm not a serial killer, am I?"

"Not really," Joe said, unable to prevent his mouth from curving into a full smile. "Keep going though. I'm enjoying watching you put your foot in your mouth." Taking a deep breath and in a move much bolder than he was used to making, he held out his hand. "I'm Joe Roberts."

"Ryan," Blue Eyes replied, shaking Joe's hand firmly. "Ryan Parker. Do you mind?" He waved a hand at the grass beside Joe.

"No, 'course not," Joe replied with a brief inclination of his head and pretended to turn his attention back to his pad. He definitely wasn't watching the way the muscles in Ryan's lithe body bunched and moved beneath his T-shirt when he took his jacket off and laid it on the ground. Neither was he openly staring when the man sat down next to him and stretched long—really long—legs out in front of him, thigh muscles swelling beneath the denim of his jeans as Ryan crossed his ankles. Although he would possibly admit to maybe dribbling just a little when Ryan lay back on his elbows and lifted his beautiful face to the sun—and he did almost drop his pencil when Ryan made a contented whimpering sound in his throat that Joe was sure could be classified as pornographic. At least his cock certainly thought so, as it suddenly stretched and took an interest in proceedings.

"Sorry?" he squeaked, feeling his cheeks grow hot when he realised that not only was Ryan speaking to him, but that he'd been caught staring.

"I assume you're an art student," Ryan repeated, with a gentle smile.

"Yes," Joe nodded, crossing his legs and laying his pad on his lap. He slipped his pencil behind his right ear and reached for the bottle of Pepsi he had in his backpack. "Second year," he explained, unscrewing the bottle and taking a swig of the now lukewarm drink. "We're covering architecture this term and my lecturer said that the best place to find beautiful craftsmanship is in a church. Especially one as old as this."

"Do you live nearby?" Ryan asked, lifting a hand to shield his gaze from the sun.

"No," Joe replied with a laugh. "I'm from Essex. Didn't the accent give me away? My mate suggested St Mary's. Apparently a family member got married here once and he remembered how beautiful the church was. I figured it must have been fantastic if Malc had noticed. What with him having his head up his own arse since 1998 when he discovered Playboy." He grinned widely. "So I drove up here this morning. Booked myself into a little B&B up the road and figured I'd spend the weekend with my sketchpad in my hand." He tilted his head questioningly. "I assume you're from around here?"

Ryan nodded. "That obvious, huh? Yeah, I'm a local boy through and through." He gazed at the angel Joe had been sketching and nodded towards her. "So what was it about her that caught your eye?" he asked.

Joe followed Ryan's gaze and smiled as he once again traced the curve of her alabaster skin in his mind. "I have a bit of a thing for angels anyway," he admitted. "But she's exquisite. I don't think I've ever seen one with so much detail on her. She looks as though she fell to Earth and was frozen in time. But at the same time, she's so lifelike it feels as though she could wake at any moment and just take flight." He blushed again when he saw the wide smile on Ryan's face. "Sorry—I tend to get a bit carried away, probably not making much sense."

"Don't apologise," Ryan retorted. "It's nice to see someone so passionate about what they love. It's not something you come across very often in this world. People give up too easily, never follow anything through. Some people never get the chance to fulfil their potential and I believe that, if you have a dream, you should grab it—live it, you know what I mean?" Ryan flushed, shrugging as he noticed the way Joe was looking at him, half-confused, half-wary, and smiled. "Sorry, you're not the only one who gets carried away." Glancing down at the sketchpad carefully balanced on Joe's lap, he held out his hand. "May I?"

Joe handed Ryan the pad and then turned to rifle through his backpack. His cheeks grew warm and an army of butterflies took flight in his stomach as he suddenly realised that this man's opinion of his work mattered to him. That it meant something. He had no idea why he felt that way, especially when, technically, Ryan was a complete stranger; he just knew with an odd certainty that it did. He turned away, pretended to study a nearby gravestone with interest, and listened to the soft rustle of the pages as Ryan turned each one carefully. *Oh, God,* Joe thought in a panic. *What if he thinks they're crap?*

"Well," Ryan said softly, closing the sketchpad and nudging Joe in the thigh with the corner of it.

"Well?" Joe echoed, turning and taking it, laying it carefully on top of his backpack. He forced himself to meet Ryan's gaze and searched the blue eyes for any negativity. "Come on, mate, you're killing me," he half-laughed when the other man didn't respond straight away.

"Give me a chance," Ryan replied with a smile. "Wow, they're brilliant, Joe. You've got a real feel for light and shadow, and I can tell you have a real understanding for the human form." He put a hand on Joe's thigh. "You're really good."

Joe looked down at the slender hand that was burning a hole through his cargo pants and swallowed against the sudden lump in his throat. Lifting his gaze, he stared into the soft blue of Ryan's eyes and slipped his tongue out to moisten his lips. "Thanks, they're alright," he said softly. Every fibre of his being wanted to lean in and close the distance between them; to press his lips to the other man's, to feel Ryan's mouth move beneath his own and to slip his tongue into—he could feel himself beginning to sway forward when Ryan removed his hand in a swift, jerky movement, startling him from his daydream. Joe straightened, his cheeks flushing yet again and quickly downed another mouthful of Pepsi. "So, are you interested in art and architecture then?" He said, desperately trying to recover what was left of his dignity.

"Yes," Ryan replied, clearing his throat and running a hand through his blond hair. "I spend a lot of time here. This place is full of history. If you like, I could show you around. Let you in on some of its deep dark secrets. If you want to, that is."

Joe felt relief flow through him at the hope in Ryan's tone and he nodded, putting his things into the backpack. "That would be great," he said enthusiastically. "My fingers were starting to cramp a bit anyway, and I could use a breather. So what delights does the church hold?"

"Now you've done it," Ryan said, dropping him a wink. "I am just full of shit, I mean information, about this place. Come, Joe Roberts, let me take you on a journey through the annals of history and take you into the depths of St Mary's. Do you know that St Mary's has five carvings of the Green Man?"

"The Green Man?" Joe queried with a smile, caught up in the childish enthusiasm on Ryan's face.

"Yep, the Green Man," he replied solemnly. "No-one actually knows where he came from but they think he was Celtic and pre-dates Christianity itself. Come on," he urged, grabbing Joe's arm and pulling him toward the huge doors of the church.

"I want to show you the Monk's Cell, which is now the library and where they keep all the parish documents. Oh, and let's not forget The Strainer."

"The Strainer?" Joe laughed, trying to ignore the churning in his stomach at the feel of Ryan's fingers clenched around his forearm. "Is there a tearoom in there as well then?"

"Very funny, Essex boy," Ryan retorted, pushing Joe ahead of him and into the church. "The Strainer, I'll have you know, is the arch that holds the church up. It's not something you Essex folk pour your PG through."

"Essex boy?" Joe huffed, poking Ryan in the side in retaliation as they entered the church. "Well, maybe you should speak a bit clearer, you know, what with you being from up North an' all."

"Up North?!" Ryan shook his head and laughed loudly, a deep rich sound that echoed around the high ceilings of the building. "We're in the Midlands, you wally."

"It's up North to me," Joe grinned back. "Come on then, when does the tour start? I don't think much of the guide so far."

"Oh, I'll give you a tour all right," Ryan said with another wink. "Now pay attention."

▲

BY THE TIME Ryan's inventive and humorous tour of St Mary's had finished, the sun was low in the sky and Joe's stomach was growling like a grizzly bear. "I suppose I should be getting back," he said reluctantly, glancing up at the sky. "It's too dark to get any more sketching done today."

"Plus your stomach thinks your throat's been cut," Ryan observed with a chuckle when another grumble slipped out into the stillness around them.

"Very funny," Joe replied, poking Ryan in the side and grinning when the other man yelped. He lifted his backpack higher onto his shoulder and held out his hand. "Well, I guess I'm gonna go. Thanks for the tour, and the company. Maybe I'll see you tomorrow?" He tried to keep the pathetic hopefulness out of his tone, not wanting to sound like a complete twat with his first crush.

"I'm usually around," Ryan replied, clasping Joe's fingers in his, not shaking them, but just holding them in a gentle grip.

"'Bye then," Joe replied, his gaze dropping to the perfect bow of Ryan's mouth. He didn't think he had ever wanted to kiss someone as badly as he wanted to kiss Ryan right now. But he knew he wouldn't. He wasn't that brave. Good grief no, he was far too polite to make the first move. Not that he would have had a chance, because in a movement so quick that Joe barely registered it, Ryan dropped his fingers and walked away. Joe felt a bit like a lovesick girl as he watched him leave, but he couldn't look away—not yet—and he felt a flutter deep in his belly when Ryan turned and waved before he slipped through the side gate in the far wall.

▲

LYING ON HIS bed in the B&B, his stomach now full of the steak and chips he'd had down at the local pub, Joe stared at the sketches he had made of Ryan that day. Even if he did say so himself, he had captured the other man perfectly. The high cheekbones, the firm jaw and those full lips. He'd even managed to detail the swirl of Ryan's hair as it curled around his face and lay across his shoulders, the soft tendrils flicking up. Joe smiled as he remembered teasing Ryan about his flowing locks. He lifted his hand to trace the pencil drawing with his fingers, and wished that he'd had the nerve to touch the smooth skin it depicted.

"Yeah, right," he sighed heavily. "Like that was ever gonna happen. He was way out of my league." *So you're not going back there tomorrow to see him?* A little voice whispered. *Oh, of course, it's the angel you're going back for.* "Shut up," Joe huffed, closing his sketchpad and rubbing a hand across his eyes. He was debating whether to run himself a bath when there was a soft knock at the door. Getting up, he put his sketchbook on top of the chest of drawers and opened it. He couldn't prevent the gasp that fell from his lips when he looked into soft blue eyes. "Ryan?"

"Hey," Ryan's smile was hesitant. He ran a hand through his hair. "Can I come in?" He glanced up and down the hall. "I sneaked past the desk."

"Of course, sorry, come in," Joe's words fell over each other and he found himself grabbing Ryan's arm and dragging him into the room, quickly closing the door behind him. "What are you doing here?" He could have kicked himself. "I mean, hi," he trailed off.

"I'm sorry," Ryan began, his expression suddenly unsure and he turned towards the door. "I shouldn't have come. I read this wrong. I'm sorry, I'll go."

"No!" Joe blushed brilliantly at his own exclamation and grasped Ryan's forearm. "I just wasn't expecting to see you."

"Thank God," Ryan said on a nervous laugh, closing the gap between them. "*Did* I read this wrong?" he asked softly, lifting a hand and tracing the curve of Joe's jaw. "Come on, mate, you're killing me."

Joe grinned when his own words were thrown back at him and he slid his fingers into Ryan's thick blond hair. "Give me a chance," he teased, the butterflies in his belly flying free. "No, you *didn't* read it wrong." Amazed at his own boldness, Joe leant forwards and pressed his lips to Ryan's. It was a barely there kiss, just a brush of soft skin against soft skin, but he felt it everywhere.

"Thank God," Ryan repeated, his hands spanning Joe's lean waist. "Because I haven't been able to stop thinking about you."

Joe's eyes fluttered shut when Ryan's mouth met his. He moaned deep in his throat at the gentle swipe of Ryan's tongue, and he parted his lips, revelling in the warmth of the muscle as it caressed his. "Me neither," he rasped, breaking the kiss and then diving in again.

"You're so beautiful," Ryan groaned, running his hands down over the curve of Joe's ass, squeezing the firm globes that conformed to his palms, grinding their hips together. "I wanted you the moment I saw you. With your nose all wrinkled up, and your tongue sticking out of the side of your mouth while you sketched, I just had to have you."

"You have no idea how much I wanted this today, how many times I wanted to touch you," Joe mumbled against the skin of Ryan's throat. He bit-kissed down the length of Ryan's neck and licked at the fluttering pulse beneath his tongue, smiling as Ryan's whimper vibrated against his lips. He sucked the flesh into his mouth, the whimper turning into a cry. "Jesus!" he yelped, a shiver flowing up his spine when Ryan's hands slipped beneath the hem of his shirt and onto his bare skin. "Your hands are cold," he complained, wriggling under their touch.

"Sorry," Ryan replied with a waggle of his eyebrows as he walked Joe back towards the bed. "Think you can warm me up, Essex boy?"

"Definitely," Joe whimpered softly, as the other man lowered him onto the mattress and covered Joe's body with his own. It felt as though their clothing disappeared and within moments they were a mass of tangled limbs on the bed. Ryan's hands and lips were everywhere at the same time; kissing, touching and tantalising every erogenous zone Joe possessed and a few that he didn't know he had. *Whose belly button is an erogenous zone for fuck's sake?* Quite frankly he didn't care because the way Ryan's tongue was dipping into and lapping around his right now was sending shock waves straight to his cock.

By the time he felt Ryan's soft breath flowing in short puffs across his engorged flesh, he was desperately trying to hold onto his sanity. "Jesus, Ryan, please," he heard the plea in his voice and didn't care. When he felt the first circle of Ryan's tongue around the head of his already leaking cock, his hands clenched the bedspread he was lying on and he couldn't have prevented the involuntary jerk of his hips if he'd had a gun held to his head. Ryan's groan of satisfaction vibrated through Joe's shaft when the other man swallowed him down to the root, and Joe cried out harshly, panting through parted lips.

"Oh, my God," he whimpered. "I want you so much." Ryan released Joe's cock and slid back up his body, bringing their mouths together in a hot and dirty kiss, tongues duelling for dominance, hands whispering across soft skin. "Can I ride you?" he gasped, gazing into Joe's deep green eyes. "I need you inside me, Joe."

"Yes," Joe moaned. "Oh, God, yes. I haven't got any lube," he mumbled, biting on his lower lip when Ryan fisted him slowly.

"Don't need it," Ryan panted. "I want to feel every second. Want to feel you forever."

"Jesus," Joe said on a rush of breath. He didn't think he had ever heard anything so sexy in his entire life. He reached for his wallet on the bedside table. Inside he quickly found the condom he was desperately hoping was still in there and tossed the wallet onto the floor. He fumbled with the condom packet and ripped it open with his teeth. Joe held his breath when Ryan took the latex sheath and rolled it down his shaft. He tried not to lose it just from the look on Ryan's face as he straddled Joe's hips and reached behind him to hold him steady. "Holy fuck," he rasped when he felt the head of his cock stretch the other man wide and slide slowly inside dark heat.

"Joe, *fuck*," Ryan moaned, lowering himself inch by inch until Joe was completely inside him. "Feels so good."

"Wow," Joe breathed, gazing up at Ryan. He had never seen anything so beautiful in his entire life. The tendons were standing out in sharp relief in Ryan's neck and his head was thrown back in ecstasy, his eyes closed and his blond hair in sweaty disarray around his face.

"You should see yourself right now," he smiled, his hands sliding up Ryan's thighs and curling around his cock. "Are you ready?" he asked as he fisted Ryan's cock in firm strokes. At the brief inclination of Ryan's head, Joe planted his feet on the mattress and thrust gently, trying not to lose it immediately at the mere sight of the other man above him. He set up a rhythm that was comfortable for both of them and Ryan was soon meeting him thrust for thrust with abandon, his hands resting on Joe's chest as he bounced on his cock.

"Fuck, Joe…shit…I'm gonna come," Ryan moaned, his dazed blue eyes locking with green. "Oh, God."

Joe's wrist twisted with every stroke on Ryan's weeping shaft. He whimpered at the pure ecstasy on the other man's face. "Do it. I want to watch you come. Come on, Ryan. Fuck!" His hips lost their rhythm when Ryan pulsed hot and hard across his fingers and belly and his orgasm was literally dragged from him when Ryan's ass clamped down on him. Joe's arm slid around Ryan's shoulders. Ryan buried his face in Joe's neck, his breath hot and heavy on the sensitive skin.

"Holy shit," Joe said eloquently, Ryan's soft hair tickling his cheek.

"Uh-huh," Ryan muttered into Joe's neck and eased himself off the softening flesh inside him. He collapsed onto the mattress beside Joe and laid his blond head on the other man's chest, his arm firmly across Joe's waist. "Thank you," he whispered, kissing Joe tenderly. Stripping off the condom, he tossed it into the bin by the bed. "That was perfect."

"You weren't so bad yourself," Joe chuckled and, when he felt Ryan move slightly, pulled him in close. "Stay," he said softly, swallowing a yawn as his eyes drifted shut.

"For as long as I can," Ryan whispered back.

▲

JOE'S EYELIDS FLUTTERED and slowly opened, his hand reaching out for Ryan, but coming into contact with cold, empty sheets. He sat up and rubbed his eyes, listening for the sound of the shower, but only hearing the birds tweeting on the tree outside the window. Ryan was gone. Joe sighed, unable to help the disappointment that washed over him, until he noticed his sketch pad on Ryan's pillow, open at the sketch he had done of the other man yesterday. His lips curved in a smile when he read the inscription beneath Ryan's smiling face. *Live the dream.* Throwing back the duvet, he grabbed his clothes and headed for the bathroom.

▲

AFTER WOLFING DOWN his breakfast at a rate of knots, Joe grabbed his stuff and ran all the way down the hill to the church. He held onto the stone wall and tried to force air into his lungs, one arm held against his side where a stitch was stabbing at him.

Inside the churchyard he sat down on the grass in front of the angel and picked up his pad. He knew Ryan would turn up, he *knew* it, he just didn't know when. Joe looked up at the beautiful statue and began to continue the sketch he had started yesterday, concentrating on the flow of her skirt and the slender toes poking out from underneath the hem, while he waited.

It was just like yesterday. Joe didn't know how long he'd been sketching away in his own little world, but when the shadow fell across his pad, he dropped his pencil and his gaze flew up to meet blue eyes. Except they weren't blue and they didn't belong to Ryan.

"Hello there." The man looked to be in his early sixties. He had a broad smile on his weathered face as he looked down at Joe. "I saw you here yesterday. I was working over on the far side," he said, motioning with his hand in the opposite direction. "We get a lot of you artist types in the summer." His brown eyes gazed at the angel and his smile became wistful. "She's quite a beauty, ain't she." It wasn't a question. "Such a shame."

"A shame?" Joe asked, getting to his feet. "What do you mean?"

"The young lad who sculpted her," the man replied. "Local

lad. So much talent, so much promise. She was his final piece. Won a prize for her you know. 'Course his parents collected it, you know, what do they call it—posthumously." He sighed heavily, reached into his pocket for his handkerchief and blew his nose. "Had cancer, he did. Such a nice lad, met him once or twice myself. This is where he'd wanted the lady to stand, so after he was gone, they scattered his ashes and put her right where he'd sit and do his drawings. Just like you're doing now." He stretched and blew his nose once more. "Anyway. Me standing here gabbing all day won't get the grass cut, now will it? I'll leave you to it."

"Thank you," Joe said, gazing at the angel with new eyes. Now that he knew the story behind her, he could see the sculptor's longing for life in every curl of her hair, in every feather on her wing. Life that he knew he wouldn't have for long. The artist's passion for his craft seemed to shine with renewed vigour from every curve. Joe looked at her face and felt an undeniable stinging behind his eyes. The man, whoever he was, must have accepted his fate by the time he'd reached her face. The utter serenity and peace moulded into the stone was heartbreakingly palpable. Joe walked over and crouched down in front of her, moving the blades of grass that had grown up around the plinth, hoping the artist had signed his work, so that he could Google him when he got home.

Joe's cry broke the stillness of the air. His legs turned to jelly and his hand dropped from the plinth as the world tipped around him. Falling back onto his arse, he stared in utter disbelief at the words on the white stone.

Chiselled into the plinth were a name, a date and a simple inscription.

Ryan Parker
11.03.1979 to 18.07.2001
"Live the Dream for Me"

Joe re-read the words over and over, until he could barely see them through his tears. His head was spinning. *What? How? What?* He had no idea how this had happened. How or why he had been able to spend those few precious hours with Ryan Parker. But he knew one thing. He would do as Ryan asked and live the dream…for both of them.

▲

About Lisa Worrall

LISA IS A single mother of two small children and has been writing in one form or another since she had to attend the Head Teacher's office for her first gold star in composition. She lives in a seaside town in Essex that boasts the longest pier in the world, which is her only claim to fame. She tries valiantly, and usually without much success to balance her children, a part-time job and writing within the twenty-four hours that there are in a day. She is currently petitioning for a few extra to be added, but hasn't heard from Greenwich yet.

She's an incurable romantic at heart and loves the feeling of bringing together two people who are meant to be, even if it is only in her head. Although she does have a little sadistic streak that cannot always guarantee a happy ever after…

Facebook: facebook.com/profile.php?id=100002377395650
Twitter: @Lisa_Worrall
Goodreads: goodreads.com/author/show/3501047.Lisa_Worrall
Blog: lworrall.blogspot.com
Email: lisaworrall69@gmail.com

Silent Witness
by Anna Marie May

THE SKIES WERE heavy, the dark clouds hanging low. He stood on top of a hill, overlooking the land, one hand held out, trying to reach out to them, to squeeze them, to make them rain. It would befit his mood if the land around him were soaking wet, crying with all its might because if he had the ability, he would quite literally cry up a storm.

Davin was missing; he had been gone for twelve hours and even though the Garda were still looking for him, he knew it was unlikely he would be found alive.

His lover wasn't the sort to go on a pub crawl and to not come home. He never drank until he passed out and even if he had for once let go of everything, twelve hours was more than enough time for him to sober up. So despite not enough time having passed he had raised the alarm, hoping for the Garda, for his friends and family, to find his lover, but so far, everyone had come up empty.

Davin was a fisherman; all his family worked on or near the sea and with his boat gone, the search and rescue had shifted their focus from land to the ocean.

But no, Davin was gone. Liam felt it in his bones.

He had come back to the Drombeg stone circle because this was where they had first made love the night they met, just half a year ago. Some might say their whirlwind romance would soon burn out, it couldn't possibly last, but Liam had known better. Some things, some core truths, wouldn't change with time, and finding his one and true love was one of them.

He narrowed his eyes, staring into the distance, watching as the sun slowly sank lower, its fiery red ball slowly vanishing beneath the Irish Sea. Memories arose just as the fog started rolling in from the sea, and Liam closed his eyes, allowing them to overtake him.

For now, memories were all he had of Davin.

He closed his eyes, letting the sinking sun and the promise of rain hanging heavily in the air pull him back to that first night together, six months ago.

▲

THEY STUMBLED ALONG the path, unsure where they were going but drawn by an invisible force to keep on going. They had left the pub an hour ago and by now they were out in the middle of nowhere with nothing but sheep to keep them company.

"Where are we going?" Davin grumbled. With an eye roll, Liam answered, "To find a place to fuck."

Something tugged at his hand and with a frown, Liam stopped to turn around.

"Then why are we still walking?"

"To find…"

"Yes…yes," Davin replied with a faint tone of annoyance, "I know, to find a place to fuck."

Liam tilted his head sideways, wondering where this was going.

"Has it occurred to you that we're already out in the middle of nowhere? Where else would you like to go?"

"Um…"

"And why didn't we go back to my place?"

Liam blinked, not sure why they hadn't done that and in the end he settled for a shrug.

"I like it here," was the only answer he could think of. The stone circle had always held a special significance for Liam and for some reason even he couldn't put into words, he had wanted to bring Davin here, to show him this place. Crazy really if he thought about it. Of course Davin had been here before, how could he not have been? But logic wasn't always what drove him, well sometimes you just had to go with your feelings, with your instincts.

The spell was broken when, with a few choice curses, Davin launched himself at Liam.

His strong hands grabbed Liam by his neck, hauling him close and then their lips met in a heated kiss.

Something rattled in the bushes but the men ignored it. There were no snakes in Ireland and any other furry creature surely had better things to do than to stay and watch.

Davin nibbled on his tongue while Liam moved in closer, pushing his tongue into Davin's mouth, tasting beer and some of the crackers they'd had earlier on. He didn't mind though because this was Davin, and although their acquaintance could only be measured in hours so far, Liam suspected that nothing about Davin could ever be anything but endearing.

His hands came to rest on his lover's hips, fingers slowly inching underneath the shirt until they found warm skin. His hands roamed higher; Davin grunted into their kiss, pulling at Liam's clothes, and because Liam was an agreeable sort he lifted his hands, allowing Davin to pull his shirt over his head.

"Love your skin," Davin mumbled, and to prove his point he started to nibble along Liam's jaw, planting soft kisses until he buried his head in the crook of Liam's neck, inhaling deeply.

"What are you doing?" Liam wondered, holding on to Davin, shifting his feet so that he could push one leg in between the other man's legs.

Liam's cock was already on the way to being painfully hard but when Davin twisted, humping forward and pushing his own erection into Liam's, he couldn't help the low whimper that escaped him.

"Smelling you," Davin answered, and with a snort Liam let

it go. Davin was an odd sort of man, and if smelling Liam was going to make him happy, then who was he to deny him that?

"We didn't bring anything," Davin lamented, slowly pulling away until his dark eyes could meet Liam's in the star lit sky.

The night sky was clear and the stars were all the light they needed.

Liam chuckled. "Guess we didn't plan this right."

"*We* didn't plan anything," Davin shot back, putting emphasis on the first word. "You dragged me out of the pub and instead of going home, you brought me all the way out here."

"You could've said something!" Liam countered because Davin was usually pretty vocal about the things he didn't want to do. If he truly hadn't wanted to come this way, he would've made himself known.

He more felt than saw the other man shrugging in the night, "I guess I was curious."

And having said that he pushed Liam back until he was lying on the ground. Rocks dug into his back but he didn't mind, because moments later Davin's warm body settled on top of him and then nimble fingers unfastened his trousers, pulling out his cock.

His back arched while his hips rode up to meet Davin's hands.

His own hands came to rest once again on his lover's hips, holding on as if his life depended on it. There was more rustling of clothes, a zipper undone and then Davin took both their cocks into his hands.

Davin had strong hands; big hands and he made good use of them, working both of them until Liam no longer knew who he was or where he was.

His body tingled, nerve endings he hadn't known existed firing at top speed like a supernova.

"Davin!" he screamed, his word echoing through the night and for a moment only silence greeted him. The world seemed to have stopped around him; the leaves were no longer rustling in the wind, the sheep had gone quiet and an eerie silence hung heavy in the air.

Then Davin broke the spell by shouting Liam's name, collapsing on top of Liam and trapping both of their spent cocks between their bodies.

They should move; staying like this was a bad idea. He could already feel the cold of the night seeping into his body and the evidence of their lovemaking was rapidly cooling on their bellies.

Still, neither one of them moved and when daylight broke, Liam discovered they had made it to the stone circle before succumbing to their passions. Last night he had been sure they were close, but under the night's sky he had been unable to judge the distance accurately.

The Drombeg stone circle stood majestically around them. A testament of a past long forgotten and now a silent witness to their love.

▲

TEARS STREAMED DOWN Liam's face, wetting his cheeks but since the heavens had finally broken, he didn't notice. The land around him was drowning in a torrent of rain. The heavy drops were blanketing the world, shielding him from whoever was out there, making it easy for him to believe that he was the only living soul around for miles.

Davin was gone; lost at sea, yet another victim claimed by the heavy waters, but his memory would always live in Liam's heart.

He knelt in front of the stones, pulling out the pocket knife he had hidden in the back of his jeans.

The stones had stood witness before, and now he was going to make sure no one would ever forget his lover.

It wasn't easy to etch their names into the stone, but he had nowhere else to be and he was fuelled by a maelstrom of love and anger. Love for Davin and what they had shared, and anger because he had been taken from him way too soon.

L&D were here.

There, he was done.

An Irish story is a sad story, his grandmother had once told him, and only now did he understand the true meaning behind her words.

Davin, he thought, I love you. I'll never forget you and the stones will be our witness. Till the end.

▲

About Anna Marie May

ANNA MARIE MAY lives in the South of Ireland where rolling hills and stormy seas are a fact of life. She started writing at the age of fifteen and her inspiration comes from her grandmother's stories about elves and goblins lurking in the woods outside of her home.

Writing is a way for her to blow off steam, to create new worlds and to visit them in her dreams. Her first novel was published by Dreamspinner Press (*Green Lake*) in 2010 and her newest novel, *Love For Hire*, will be available in autumn of 2011. Juggling life and many new projects is never easy but hopefully there shall be many more books coming up in the near future.

Website: annamariemay.com

Sweet Temptation
by Jennie Caldwell

AT THE SOUND of the mower, Philip looked up from his usual head-down-scurry up the path to the church. *Oh, good Lord, the devil's tempting me today!* It was the young man from the council, back again to mow the grass in the churchyard. Except that, this week, the hot July sun had enticed the man to remove his shirt. Philip stared at the flesh on display. Sleek muscles, firm but not too bulky, were damp with sweat and covered in a fine sheen of dust and bits of grass. There was a smear of mud which extended over one side of his chest, grazing the underside of his left nipple. The man's dark, tousled hair was damp too and sticking to his neck. He was wearing jeans which looked soft with repeated wear over long legs. Philip couldn't see the back view, but knew from past sightings that the man had the perfect arse. He was perfect all over, in fact.

Philip swallowed; his mouth and throat suddenly devoid of moisture. At that point the man looked up from the mower and a thrill of embarrassment shot through Philip as he realised that he'd been caught staring. He jerked his head down and began to hurry up the path once more.

"Hey, wait!"

Philip stopped and turned to face the man again, dreading

what would more than likely be an unpleasant scene. Instead of the expected angry expression, the man approached him with an open, even friendly look on his face as he made his way past the gravestones towards Philip.

There was a moment of awkwardness when the man reached him as both stared cautiously at each other and Philip tried desperately to keep his eyes on the man's face and not that almost-mud-smeared nipple. Finally the man broke the silence.

"Hi."

"Hello."

"I've seen you about a bit when I've been here. Are you the Vicar?"

"Not unless I've changed gender. "

"Pardon?"

Philip took pity on the man. He wasn't quite sure why he was being so short with him, especially as he was only trying to be friendly. If he was being honest with himself it was probably because he felt a bit threatened by all the masculine beauty in front of him. His own thin body and average looks were nothing compared to all that gorgeous hair, toned muscle and dark nipples.

Stop thinking about his nipples!

"The Vicar is a lady. I'm the Verger, which is why I'm here quite a lot of the time."

The poor man looked even more puzzled now. He'd probably never heard of a Verger. Philip gave an inward sigh over the ignorance of society when it came to church matters. "The Verger is…"

"I know what a Verger is."

"Oh, all right then. It's just you looked a bit confused and I assumed that you didn't know what one was."

"I *was* confused."

The man smiled. Philip stared. Could the man get any lovelier? His mouth was wide and inviting, his teeth white and straight. Philip wanted to kiss that smile, to see that smile directed at him in a post coital haze.

Stop it!

The man carried on speaking, jerking Philip out of his illicit fantasies.

"I was confused because my mental image of a Verger is a fusty old man wearing a suit and you're nothing like that. You're…" The man hesitated, dropped his chin and looked up at Philip from under his fringe.

"I'm…"

"Well…erm…don't take this the wrong way, but you're hot."

Philip felt his mouth drop open and snapped it shut. He also, much to his complete disgust, felt his face heating up with embarrassment. How was he to reply to that? He couldn't. He had to escape. He darted a longing look at the door to the church. It would be cool in there on his heated skin. There would be peace and quiet and no young men trying to tempt him with their grime smeared nipples and beautiful smiles.

"Er…well…erm…excuse me."

Philip made a dash to the church, ignoring the man's startled "Hey! Wait!" behind him. At last he reached the door, safety was in sight. Philip turned the handle. Locked. Of course it was; it was always locked. Philip fumbled in his pocket for his keys, cursing the tight jeans he was wearing. Just as the metal bit into his fingers, he felt a hand on his shoulder and he swung around to face the man again.

Philip was gratified to see that the man was red in the face too, although whether that was due to embarrassment or sprinting up the path in the hot weather was anyone's guess. The man was right up in his personal space, breathing heavily. This close, Philip could see that he had brown eyes to match his dark hair. He could also smell him: a mixture of grass and sun and good clean sweat which made Philip want to lean in further so he could take a huge lungful of the delightful aroma. Instead he took a step back, wanting the space to think, rather than just react.

"Did I misread you?" The man's brow furrowed. "You were definitely checking me out. Definitely."

What could Philip say? He *had* been staring and the man had seen the lust in his eyes. The question was: was he going to deny it, repel the gorgeous man and go back to the safety of his quiet life?

"Erm…" Philip's brain stuttered, unable to form words in his panicked jumble of emotions.

Perhaps the man saw the confusion on Philip's face because he stepped forward again, all loose limbs, and raised his grass stained hand for Philip to shake. "I'm Nathan."

And now he had a name to go with the fantasy. It was a good name. A biblical name, if you took the longer version of Nathanael: the man who declared that Jesus was the Son of God before all the other disciples. Philip shook off that thought. He did not want to be thinking of Jesus at this moment, even if he was standing in the shadow of the church door on a hot July afternoon knowing that in a few moments he would be inside preparing the sacraments for this evening's mid week communion service. Uncertainty crept into Philip's mind and all the old arguments started to bleed in from the dark places in his mind.

It's wrong. It's a sin. I'm evil for lusting after this bright angel of a man.

The hand that Nathan was holding up started to shake a little and Philip wondered if Nathan was nervous. What an odd thing, to be nervous about him of all people. Or maybe he'd been so lost in his thoughts that he'd left it too long to return the handshake and the poor man didn't know whether to drop his hand or not. Feeling a little foolish, Philip reached out and their hands clasped.

"I'm Philip."

"Nice to meet you, Philip."

Nathan smiled that wonderful smile again and the shadows in Philip's mind began to recede in the blast of warmth he felt from both the smile and the firm calloused hand in his. He marvelled at the difference from his own smooth, pale hands and his concerns began to melt away. How could this be wrong when even holding another man's hand felt so right?

Realising that he was still holding Nathan's hand, Philip let go feeling suddenly flustered.

"Nice to meet you too. I…I'm sorry if I wasn't polite just now. You see…" Philip trailed off. Did Nathan see? He was obviously a very confident young man to be able to declare himself like that. Philip had never…he wouldn't dare…but how *freeing* it must feel to step out like that. Without fear.

I want that. I want to be free.

The thought startled Philip and he stepped back again, his back pressing to the church door. He felt the coolness of the wood seep into his shirt, making him shiver despite the warm air.

Nathan watched him shiver and the smile on his face dimmed to mere politeness. He stepped away from Philip, as though to give him space, and Philip felt a coldness sweep through him that had nothing to do with the door.

"Yes, I do see. Well, sorry for disturbing you," Nathan looked over his shoulder at the mower before turning back, all trace of the smile gone now, a lingering flush in his cheeks. "I'd best get back to work then. No doubt I'll see you around." He turned and started to make his way down the church steps.

For a moment Philip was paralysed with indecision. Should he leave, just slip into the church and get on with his life in safety? But what was so great about his so-called safe life? Philip thought of his plans for the rest of the day. The peace he would find in the communion service followed by what would be a lonely evening in his flat, trying and probably failing not to think of Nathan; of missed opportunities; of what could have been the start of something exciting, thrilling; of soft lips, hard muscle, lazy smiles and dirt smeared nipples.

Stop him, you idiot!

Philip surprised himself by calling out, "Nathan, wait!"

Nathan hesitated half way down the steps, but then carried on.

"Please, Nathan."

He stopped and Philip caught up with him on the second

to last step. A flash of panic shot through Philip. What was he doing? What was he supposed to say now? His gaze roamed around the church yard, coming to rest on the largest gravestone: a huge cross, delicately carved with Celtic knotwork. He thought about all that the cross represented for him, his faith, his life and then he looked helplessly at Nathan who was standing in front of him looking sun-kissed and handsome, his brown eyes wary. Suddenly Philip felt anger mixed with a sense of despair. It shouldn't be a choice. Why couldn't he have his faith *and* Nathan? If the Bible was right, which it most surely was, and the God he worshipped was a loving and generous Father, then he surely wouldn't want his child to be lonely, to be so…bloody miserable.

All this thinking had taken too long. Nathan shook his head in obvious exasperation and disappointment.

"Look, it's fine. Honestly. I was just here to mow the grass and seeing you looking at me earlier…well, you know, something just clicked in my head and I really felt quite strongly that I should take a chance that this time you would talk to me instead of just pretending I'm not there, like you have all the other times I've been here. It was like, I don't know, fate or something"

Philip listened with astonishment as his brain tried to process what Nathan had said .

Something just clicked…felt quite strongly…take a chance…fate or something.

And suddenly it came to him. This wasn't fate and Nathan wasn't a sin. He was a gift. Philip was a good and faithful servant who had been given an unexpected gift by the Father who loves him. Before Nathan could walk away, Philip reached out and took Nathan's hand once again, but this time it was not a handshake but a caress, an overture. Philip opened his mouth and spoke, his voice hoarse.

"I'm sorry. You must think me the most cowardly of men. It's just that you've surprised me. You're so gorgeous and I…I'm just not used to…well," he waved his free hand down his body, "I mean look at me!"

Nathan's eyes followed Philip's movement with interest and his gaze came to rest at their joined hands. He ran his thumb over Philip's knuckles.

Looking up, he smiled, warming Philip to his toes.

"Yes, look at you." His eyes gleamed with admiration as he started to close the gap between them. Inches away from Philip's lips he said, "I'd really like to kiss you. May I?"

Philip's heart was suddenly pounding so hard that he was lightheaded. Not trusting his voice, he nodded slowly.

Nathan leaned in, all glorious muscle and sweat and sweet, sweet temptation and kissed Philip softly, just a brush of lips.

Thank you, Lord!

They pulled away and looked into each other's eyes, one set filled with a burgeoning hope, the other wide with astonished delight. This time it was Philip who smiled, wide and welcoming at this gift, this new beginning, and kissed Nathan back. Right there on the steps to the church.

⋏

About Jennie Caldwell

MORE KNOWN FOR reviewing books than writing them, Jennie Caldwell decided that the lure of short fiction was too great and so has dangled her toes into the waters of m/m romance. A Yorkshire lass through and through, Jennie lives near Bronte Country with a husband, four children and two cats.

A Matter of Opinion
by Mara Ismine

RICK COULDN'T STAND it any longer; Alf was sounding off again and this time it was about a couple who were refused adoption because of their religious beliefs, which wouldn't allow them to 'condone' homosexuality. Alf was a narrow minded bigot and was always ranting about something, but today Rick couldn't just shrug it off and ignore it.

The door to the staff room closed behind him cutting off Alf's vitriolic words. Rick tried to calm down and forget Alf and his stone age attitude to everything. There was still twenty minutes of lunch break left and Rick didn't want to go back to work. Maybe some fresh air would help him wipe away the slimy residue of Alf's words.

Rick slipped out of the side door into the yard and followed the faded yellow paint of the designated walkway down to the far end. He could hide behind the wood stacks until he got his temper back under control; there was plenty of room to pace and he could rant without anyone hearing him.

"Fucking bigoted arsehole!" Rick snarled. He wrapped his arms around his middle and wished he'd stopped to get his coat; the sun might be shining, but the wind was bitter and the stacks weren't offering much protection. It was all Alf's fault. "Where does he get off spouting all that crap? One of these days I'll give him a knuckle sandwich to chew on."

"I wouldn't do that," a voice said quietly. "That's instant

dismissal, you know."

Rick could feel his face flaming as he turned slowly to find the source of the voice. Couldn't he even vent in peace? He suppressed a groan as the speaker came into view; it had to be Steve, the hot driver who had featured in many of Rick's more intimate fantasies.

Rick hadn't really spoken to Steve before, but his fantasies didn't involve much in the way of conversation. He had seen enough of the driver's body to fuel his imagination, especially in summer when Steve wore shorts and tight vests. Steve had great legs with firm muscles and a light dusting of dark hair; even his knees looked good. His arms were smoothly muscled and his chest was broad. Steve looked good all over as far as Rick could tell. But it was that wide, sensuous mouth that Rick spent the most time thinking about—particularly Steve's mobile mouth giving the best blowjob ever.

Rick had an inadvertent mental replay of a favourite fantasy of his: Steve's head bobbing up and down, with those lush lips spread around his prick; followed by another frequent wish-fulfilment image of licking Steve's impressive chest. It was embarrassing to meet the man with all those thoughts in the back of his mind.

Steve had made himself a bench between two of the stacks by the simple placement of a plank. He had a vacuum flask on one side and was eating fish and chips out of the paper. The makeshift seat looked a lot better than the stuffy, Alf-infested break room, and it was out of the wind; Steve's shoulder length hair wasn't blowing around to Rick's disappointment. That hair was always dishevelled in his fantasies, but from his fingers rather than the wind.

Rick realised Steve would be expecting a response. "Yeah, I know." He rubbed a hand over his face and sighed. "But sometimes it would almost be worth losing my job just to shut him up."

"Must be Alf you're on about. What's got his knickers in a twist this time?"

"Them." Rick pointed to the newspaper folded up beside Steve where the indignant couple were front page headlines.

"Them?" Steve glanced at the colour photo. "For or against?"

"Respectable God-fearing people should get to adopt." Rick quoted in a fair imitation of Alf. Thinking of Alf was an effective antidote to the arousal that being around Steve generated.

"Bet he wouldn't be saying that if they were a respectable Muslim or Jewish couple," Steve said, staring at the photo. "I'm surprised that he got past the fact that they aren't white."

Rick was surprised by that himself. Alf was an equal-opportunity bigot and hated everyone who wasn't white, English and C of E—and if they were too rich, or benefit scroungers, or homosexuals, or females, or cat owners, they got into the hate category as well; Alf didn't approve of too many people, really.

"I'd rather be someone he hates than someone he likes." Rick gave a wry grin.

"You got that right!" Steve laughed. "Pull up a plank and park your arse."

Why not? Rick settled on the plank next to Steve. Talking to a hot man was better than pacing and would give him more fantasy fodder. He was close enough to get a hint of Steve's body spray over the scent of sawdust and wood. It was a pleasant blend and reignited the tingle of arousal.

"Have a chip." Steve proffered the paper.

"Thanks." Rick picked the nearest chip and dipped it in the tomato sauce puddle. It gave him a foolish thrill that Steve liked his sauce the same way, in a puddle rather than striped over the chips. "Do you always lurk out here at lunchtime?"

"Depends. Some days I'm out on deliveries when I have to take a break, but usually I'm back here for my second load around lunchtime."

"It must be nice to be out on the road rather than stuck inside." Rick accepted another chip when Steve held the paper towards him.

"It has its moments, but most of the time I'm happy with my

job. What about you? You work behind the counter, don't you?"

"Usually I enjoy it. Sometimes the customers are impossible, but it is real boring when there aren't any customers at all."

"Not good for the long term job prospects that." Steve laughed. "No customers soon means no job."

"Tell me about it, I've been worried about them closing this place since the credit crunch hit." Rick shuddered.

"Me too. Things are picking up a bit now though, so we should be all right."

"Hope so. I'm surprised we made it this far."

"Don't knock it. You want some cod?" Steve shoved the greasy paper towards Rick again.

They ate in a companionable silence for a couple of minutes. "Thank God it's Friday," Rick muttered.

"Not working this weekend?" Steve asked with another grin. "You got plans?"

Rick choked on his chip and looked at Steve out of the corner of his watering eyes as Steve pounded him on the back. Why was Steve asking about weekend plans? Was Steve going to ask him out? Could he be that lucky? Was Steve's hand lingering on his back?

"Nothing in particular," Rick said once he had caught his breath. "Just lazing around."

"I'm off this weekend too. Thought I'd treat myself to a pint after work. My local shut a couple of months ago and I haven't found a replacement yet. I think I'll try the Rose and Crown today. You ever been there?"

"Once, I think."

"What's it like? Worth a visit?"

"It was a while back I was there. I think they've got new management since then."

"I'll still give it a go. You want to join me? If you aren't doing anything else. It sometimes gets a bit lonely drinking somewhere new." Steve's grin looked a bit strained, almost as though he was expecting Rick to say no.

Rick stopped the panicked rejection that was his automatic response to requests from his workmates to join them for a pint. This was Steve—and what better way of finding out if all those fantasies might have a chance of becoming reality? Rick summoned all his courage and agreed to meet Steve at the Rose and Crown after work.

They didn't get to talk more about their plans because Stan was opening the gate and lunch break was over. Rick headed back to the sales counter with his gut full of butterflies. Should he have accepted Steve's invitation? It was only for a quick drink, he told himself.

As far as Rick knew nobody at work realised he was gay. Life was simpler that way and he'd rather not deal with the likes of Alf's opinion on the subject day in and day out. Being out and proud might work in a big city, but Rick didn't think his skin was thick enough to be out and proud in a builder's merchants in a small town.

Having a pint with Steve shouldn't threaten Rick's secrets. It was just a pint, not even a date. Steve probably didn't mean anything by the invitation, other than he didn't want to drink alone. But wouldn't it be great if it was a real date?

By the time Rick pushed through the door of the Rose and Crown he wasn't sure he'd be able to drink anything without throwing up. His stomach was still full of butterflies and he almost wished he'd refused the invitation. He hoped that the alcohol would help him relax. Steve was already at the bar, and grinned as he spotted Rick.

"You made it." Steve sounded glad about Rick's arrival. "It's my round, what'll you have?"

"Lager, please." Rick moved up to the bar and looked around the pub while Steve ordered their drinks. The Rose and Crown might be under new management, but the décor was decidedly old-fashioned. It was all olde worlde beams, dark furniture and brass ornaments. The outside looked old enough that the beams might even be authentic.

There were only a handful of customers in the public bar. Three men were loosely clumped at the far end with loosened ties and half full glasses. A man and woman sat at a corner table with their heads close together, oblivious to the rest of the world. Rick looked away quickly, embarrassed by the couple's intimacy.

"Here." Steve handed Rick his lager and gestured to a table near the fire. "Let's sit over there. I can't resist a real fire."

"Not something you see very often, is it?" Rick sipped his lager and followed Steve across the room.

"Looks like this is a good place for a quiet pint." Steve savoured a mouthful of the dark bitter he had chosen. "That really hits the spot. How's your lager?"

"It's fine." Rick took another quick sip. It tasted like lager always tasted—cold and fizzy.

"Do you have a local? Or are you more of a clubber?"

"I prefer pubs to clubs," Rick forced the words out rather than make another short reply. He didn't think the question covered the places he went to occasionally in the nearest towns big enough to have gay bars. Or maybe he should mention those places? If Steve knew them then it was almost certain that he was gay. Almost. Rick could feel his face heating in another blush. "I'm not much of a drinker really," he blurted.

"I'm not much for clubs either, I have to be in the right mood to drag all that way and be deafened." Steve took another mouthful from his glass and closed his eyes as he swallowed. "I'm not much of a drinker either, despite appearances." Steve opened his eyes and put his pint down as he grinned at Rick. "This will be the only one I have," he gestured to the glass. "And only when I've got two days off."

"Sure. Your job depends on your licence, doesn't it? Not worth risking that." Rick couldn't really concentrate on anything other than the movement of Steve's throat as the beer went down. Swallowing featured in several fantasies.

"No it's not, so I just have the one."

"Only sensible," Rick said and cleared his throat to stop his voice sounding so husky. He took another sip of his lager. Was Steve watching the lager go down? Rick told himself he was just imagining the interest he wanted to see.

This was a lot more difficult than going to one of the clubs, which was why he didn't do it much. The clubs were full of anonymous men looking for a quick hook up. How was he supposed to tell if Steve was gay, let alone interested, unless Steve made a really obvious move? Rick didn't think he had the nerve himself to make that first move.

"Anyway, it's Friday and we've both got two days off so let's stop talking shop." Steve changed the subject. "That looks good." Steve was staring at something over Rick's shoulder and Rick turned to look. The young couple had ordered food and it was being served to them. It did look good and it smelt even better. Rick's stomach rumbled to remind him that he hadn't eaten much today.

"You want to try the food? Or do you need to get on?" Steve asked.

"I think my beans on toast can wait until tomorrow, and that does smell good." Rick laughed as his stomach growled an agreement.

"Beans on toast? You are living high on the hog. I think my toasted cheese sandwich can wait, as well. So what shall we have?"

Rick looked around and spotted the chalk boards above the bar with today's specials in multi-coloured letters. "Cottage pie." Rick decided. "I'll get the food as you got the drinks."

"I'll have the lasagne," Steve said. "Next time you can get the drinks and I'll get the food."

Rick couldn't stop himself smiling as he went up to the bar to order the food. He liked the idea of a 'next time'; being friends with Steve was better than nothing. And maybe it would lead to more.

"What a waste of food," Steve said, nodding towards the young couple, when Rick took his seat at the table. "Talk about love's young dream, I don't think they've touched a bite. I hope

I was never that dopey in love."

"What's the point of being in *lurve* if you don't act daft as a brush?" Rick chuckled and risked a glance at the other table. "It's a good job their friends aren't around to take photos."

"Is that what your friends did to you?"

"Yeah. And the bastards posted them on line so everyone could have a good laugh." Rick could feel himself blushing again, but at least it didn't hurt to think about it anymore. He still felt sad that he wasn't with Aaron, but the pain of being dumped had gone.

"Ouch. Are they still your friends?"

"Sort of." Rick shrugged and took a mouthful of lager to give himself time to pick his words carefully, "My ex hooked up with one of the others and things are a bit uncomfortable if I meet up with the group now."

"That's not fair. They don't seem like very good friends to cut you out in favour of your ex." Steve frowned and sounded annoyed on Rick's behalf.

"It was my decision." Rick hurried to defend his friends, even if he did agree with Steve, "I was the one that pulled away."

"And you were the one who was dumped?"

"Yeah. I was rather pathetic for a while and then it got to be a habit to avoid them. Not their fault." Rick was warmed by Steve's concern, even as he excused his friends' behaviour again.

"You need to find yourself a pretty little thing to make your ex jealous," Steve ordered rather than suggested. "You shouldn't give up on your friends like that. We all need friends."

"That might work." Rick was glad that their food arrived then and interrupted the conversation. He wished he could call Steve a 'pretty little thing' because Steve would be the ideal antidote to Aaron; and Aaron would be green with envy.

But as Steve was around six foot and had impressive muscles he didn't qualify as a 'little thing', even if some variation of 'pretty' could apply to him. Steve didn't have a washboard stomach, but Rick imagined that the little bit of padding would make a comfy spot to lay his head, and have a great view.

Rick knew what his reflection showed him every morning and it didn't rate 'pretty' even if he could be described as 'little' when compared to Steve. He wasn't ugly, but he wasn't anything special.

They tucked into the food and didn't talk much for a while as they ate. Rick had time to think and realised that he had to find out if Steve was into men, in all meanings of the word. This might be his only opportunity, despite Steve's hints about a next time. Rick would be more than happy for Steve to be into him.

Rick was still arguing with himself as he ate the final mouthful of his cottage pie. Would it be best to ask Steve if he was het? Or should Rick admit to being gay? What would he lose by letting Steve know? Maybe a potential friendship and he might have to put up with some unpleasant gossip and comments at work. But he might gain Steve.

"You seem a bit distracted," Steve said, startling Rick out of his confused thoughts. "Thinking about your ex?"

"Yes, I mean no." Rick rolled his eyes, shut his mouth and took a calming breath before trying again, "I was thinking about something, but not my ex. Or not exactly. I don't know how to go about replacing him." Rick snapped his mouth shut. He hadn't meant to out himself quite like that.

"Him? Ah. So why is it a problem to find another bloke?" Steve grinned at Rick. "You're an attractive man, so it really shouldn't be a problem."

"Oh." Rick could feel his face flaming. Steve thought he was attractive? Really? "I just don't know how to tell if another man is interested. I grew up with Aaron and we never really dated—we just were."

"No gaydar then?"

"No. Does that really exist?" Rick took a sip of lager to wash his dinner down.

"Some of my friends claim to be infallible, but it's never

been that reliable for me. I just have to work up the courage to make a pass and hope I don't get thumped."

"You're really gay?" Rick asked before he could think about it.

"Yes. Always have been." Steve was looking nervous, but he kept his eyes locked with Rick's.

"Me too. So is this a date?" Rick's heart was hammering.

"It could be a date if you want it to be."

"You don't know how much!" Rick laughed in relief.

"Do you have any rules about kissing on first dates?" Steve laughed with Rick and seemed to relax.

"Rules? I don't think so, apart from the one that says there had better be *some* kissing at least." Rick could feel his face heating again at his words, but he didn't miss the way Steve's tongue ran over his lips in response to them.

"Time to get out of here, I think." Steve lifted his glass and drained it. "Drink up and then tell me if we're going to my place or yours to discuss this in a lot more detail."

Rick tilted his glass and swallowed the last of his lager without dribbling, despite the big grin he couldn't control. He tried to remember what state his flat was in, as he did his cleaning at weekends and just tended to leave things during the week.

Had he picked up yesterday's socks or just dropped them by the sofa? Could he guarantee that his dirty underpants were in the laundry basket? Or had he left them on the bathroom floor again? Did any of that really matter if he could get his hands on Steve?

Rick followed Steve out into the car park trying not to crowd too close.

"Where are we going?" Steve stepped away from the brightly lit pub door as he asked the question. "How far away do you live?"

"About five miles," Rick said. "How about you?"

"Just round the corner." Steve grinned, the expression only just visible in the dark. "My place?"

"Yes." Rick realised that he sounded way too enthusiastic.

Didn't he want more than a quickie with Steve? The answer was instant—yes, he wanted more, but he would settle for a one night stand right now and worry about regrets in the morning. He added hastily, "If that's all right with you?"

"I wouldn't have offered if it wasn't." Steve chuckled. "Where are you parked? I walked so you can give me a lift. You might as well bring your car round to mine, rather than leave it here."

"Okay." Rick led the way to his car and unlocked it. "It feels odd to drive a professional driver. It's a bit like a driving test."

"Just get us to my place in one piece. I've got better things to think about than how well you drive a car." Steve walked around and got in the passenger seat.

Rick slid into the driver's seat and turned to look at Steve, "That doesn't help, you know?"

"No?" Steve chuckled and gave Rick a heated look. The interior light clicked off and Steve leaned closer. "How about this?" He closed the distance between them and kissed Rick.

Steve tasted of herbs and bitter, and beneath that was the more intoxicating taste of man. Rick kissed him back, getting more of that elusive flavour.

"Any better?" Steve pulled back slightly.

"Better?" Rick struggled to make sense of the question.

"Mm. I think you should get us to my place. Now."

"Uh. Right." Rick started the engine and turned the lights on. "You'll have to give me directions."

"I can do that." Steve's voice was husky and more suggestive than Rick needed right then.

"To your place? So we can get out of the car?" Rick tried not to think about what they might do once they got that far, as he still needed to drive and get them there in one piece.

"Indoors sounds good." Steve smirked and settled back in his seat to give Rick the necessary directions. "Although I don't think that we're going to do a lot of discussing."

"Maybe later?" Rick suggested pulling up in front of a small terrace of houses.

"Much later," Steve agreed. "We've got all weekend to get to discussing stuff."

That sounded good, Rick thought, as he followed Steve to the front door. A weekend of getting to know Steve's body, and Steve, sounded a lot more appealing than grocery shopping and laundry.

Rick stopped thinking as he found himself pinned to the front door. His eyes drifted shut as he sank into the kiss.

Steve felt good everywhere they touched. Rick was enfolded in heat and that mouth was every bit as good as he'd dreamed it would be. Steve pulled him away from the door and they staggered the couple of steps to the stairs.

"House tour later," Steve pulled back long enough to say. "Settee that way. Bed this way. Choose."

"S-supplies?" Rick managed to force his swollen lips to form the word.

"This way." Steve almost growled and dragged Rick up the steep stairs to the miniscule landing. "In here. Bog opposite— don't fall down the stairs finding it in the middle of the night."

Rick nodded, amazed at how many words Steve could put together when aroused. He gave Steve's rock hard prick an extra squeeze as he translated 'the middle of the night' into meaning he was staying for breakfast.

Steve shoved the bedroom door open, flicked the light on and herded Rick towards the bed with both hands steering Rick's bum. Rick stumbled and fell onto the bed, bouncing when he hit the mattress, until Steve landed on top of him.

They rolled and fought to get face to face again and resume the interrupted kiss. Rick slid his hand back under the waistband of Steve's trousers reclaiming his prize. There wasn't room to do much more than squeeze, but even that made Steve groan and thrust against Rick.

Steve tugged at Rick's jacket and got it off one arm before burrowing his cold hands beneath Rick's sweatshirt and exploring his chest.

Rick yelped into the kiss at the shock of cold and then

pushed back against the touch, enjoying the feel of strong calloused hands stroking his skin. He freed his hand from Steve's long, silky hair and tugged at his coat, wanting to touch more than the good handful of flesh he already had. The coat didn't budge, what with both of Steve's hands occupied in mapping Rick's torso.

Rick wormed his hand between them to undo Steve's trousers and give his other hand more room to manoeuvre. Steve seemed to approve, lifting his body away from Rick's and leaving room for his trousers and underwear to be pushed down out of the way. Rick took advantage of the extra space to do more than just squeeze.

One of Steve's hands fumbled at Rick's fly and shoved Rick's clothes out of the way. They both sighed at the skin on skin contact. Steve crowded closer and lined up their dicks, grasping both to set up a fast rhythm.

Rick groaned into the now rather messy kiss they were still sharing. This wasn't something he had imagined them doing, but he was sure it would be re-lived frequently. Steve's hand felt so good, the calloused skin felt indescribable and the fast, sure pumping was driving Rick mad.

He was beyond thinking and just let his body take over, thrusting eagerly into Steve's hand and feeling his balls draw up. It did not take long for him to come, spurting between their joined hands. He hoped that his whimper sounded more like a moan outside his head. Any faint embarrassment faded as Steve followed him over the edge with a series of grunts.

The wild kiss gentled and ended slowly as they both panted for breath. Rick became aware of something sharp digging into his back where his jacket was bunched up beneath him and other discomforts that he hadn't noticed a few minutes before. Steve was a heavy weight crushing him into the mattress, and he squirmed, trying to get into a more comfortable position.

"Sorry. I'm too heavy," Steve said as he lifted up on one shaking arm. "Best we get cleaned up a bit and more comfy."

"I think I'm lying on my keys." Rick reluctantly released his hold on Steve's now limp and sticky cock.

"Best you get undressed then," Steve suggested on a stifled chuckle. "We can get into bed ready for the next round."

Rick was more than happy to agree. He wanted to explore Steve's body without clothes getting in the way and spending the night sounded good. He watched Steve stand up and reach into a basket by the door to produce a screwed up T-shirt to use as a towel.

"You look properly debauched." Steve stopped wiping his hands and moved back to the bed, his eyes fixed on Rick who hadn't moved. Steve leant down and carefully wiped Rick's sticky hand before moving to mop up the drying trails on his torso.

"I feel properly debauched." Rick peeled off his jacket and shirt and pushed them aside. He tried to kick off his trousers and underpants, but they got caught on his work boots. He sat up on the edge of the bed to untie his laces, but was distracted by Steve stripping almost within reach. Rick's mouth watered as he watched all that fine, hair-dusted skin being revealed. He couldn't wait to touch and taste. His prick stirred with interest.

"Bugger," Steve muttered as he ran into the same problem that Rick had encountered: work boots. He dropped down onto the edge of the bed beside Rick and laughed. "I can do better than this, you know. I've spent too long watching you to have any smooth moves left now you're actually here."

"Your moves are smooth enough for me." Rick blushed at saying something so wet, but how could he think of anything better when Steve had just confessed to watching him?

"Boots off!" Steve eyed Rick's cock and licked his lips.

Rick couldn't help chuckling as they bent to fight with their boots. This was going to be a great weekend.

Better than his wildest fantasies.

▲

About *Mara Ismine*

MARA ISMINE HAS been writing m/m romance exclusively for three or four years now, after many years writing mainly fantasy and sci-fi, and has had several titles published electronically by Torquere Press. This summer she will be published in print and ebook as part of an anthology of slashed fairytales from Less Than Three Press.

She lives in Suffolk with her husband, sons, and very large dog.

Website: maraismine.bravehost.com/MaraSite/MaraEnterPage.htm

Jeu d'Esprit
by Chris Smith

I SAT ON the side of the pond, my legs dangling in the cool water. Behind me, I could hear the raucous cheers of the village party as another sun-roasted English tomato lifted his cheap plastic champagne flute—replete with bargain bin bubbly—to the happy couple.

Catherine and William, I thought. How nice for them. I pushed up my trousers, gathering them around my knees, feeling my boxers crunch up between my legs, and waded a way into the pond. The mulch squelched up between my toes, and the pond-plants brushed against my calves.

If you'd asked me this time last year, I'd have told you that I'd be there, waving my little plastic flag, my arm wrapped around my own Kate—a Katelyn, three doors down from me and ever so blonde and leggy. I'd have bought her a hideous hat, and our own bottle of bargain bin, and some plastic cups and a rug, and we'd have been there in Hyde Park. If you'd asked me this time last year, I'd have also told you that a first class degree from a reputable London university and a good smattering of extracurriculars would have been enough to land me a decent job. This time last year, we were pulling out of recession. Now no one seems sure if we're about to fall back in again.

A fly landed on my nose, momentarily pulling me out of my

reverie. I tripped, tried to break my fall, and skinned my palms against something sharp. Oh, fuck.

Thanks to the recession I was unemployed, and back at home with my parents. This would probably not have been as bad if my parents had elected to stay in Guildford, where I'd grown up, gone to college, and had plenty of friends, but instead they'd decided to relocate to a small village in Cornwall. The recession had hit my father's job as well. There was no point staying in the commuter belt with an eminently saleable four bedroom house when a three bed cottage down in St Elena's could be had at a third of the price. While they'd been there for the last two years, integrating with the locals, I'd been up in town with Kate and the rest.

I don't know how they did it—I'd been down here for the last six months and knew almost no one. There were a few local lads with whom I had a nodding acquaintance across the bar— enough to sink a pint without getting a fist in the eye—and my mother had got me a volunteer position in the local charity shop, a surprisingly busy place thanks to the recession. The latter had kind of led to the distance in the former—apparently sorting clothes and sizing shoes is the sort of work that's 'only fit for poofters'. And yes, that is a direct quote.

"Hey, what's going on there? Are you okay?"

I squelched my way onto my hands and knees, and peered across the field. It was Benjamin.

"Ben. It's me. I'm fine." I called out, feeling my face flush as I remembered my sodden and scraped state. "It's me."

Now Benjamin is what you'd call a complication. He's an odd duck in the village; a painter apparently, and lives in a lovely ramshackle flint cottage about four doors down from the charity shop. He wanders around town with a half destroyed straw boater perched on his lanky blond hair, a pair of ancient tweed trousers, a formerly white dress shirt with French cuffs (no cufflinks) and tends to clutch either a sketchbook or a camera. He smiles at everyone. If I'm honest, the first time I saw him, I thought him the village idiot.

He's come into the shop a few times since then—gives us some old frames and sometimes framed sketches he's got no room for in his loft. Once he took off his boater, and I could see the bald spot on the top of his head. He smells of paper and turpentine, and slightly of cats. He's shy to the point of rudeness, but the minute he smiles, you forget all that. Benjamin has a lovely smile—his teeth may be slightly yellowed, but he smiles as if he wants to split his head in two with the joy of existence. His eyes crease up at the corners, twinkling blue, and he gets dimples in both his cheeks. When Benjamin smiles, you forget you're having an awful day, that you've got to go and size a box of elderly ladies' girdles, that some prat's just been in the shop trying to bargain his way to a deal when all the proceeds go to charity. When Benjamin smiles, you forget the email you've just read, where Kate says she's breaking up with you because she's found a nice bloke who works in the city. When Benjamin smiles, the world is just a better place.

As you can probably tell from that maudlin rambling, Benjamin has caused me some confusion. I'd been to a mixed day-school, so I'd never felt the need for the type of companionship that some of my public school friends assure me was de rigueur, and at university there'd been enough women—and after meeting Kate I'd not felt the need to look any further. But now, now I'd re-do the display window twice a week, in the hopes of catching Benjamin wandering up and down the street. I'd taken to smoking, so I'd have an excuse to loiter outside. I'd said maybe seven words to the bloke in the last six months, and yet my day was centred around seeing him.

You'd think I'd have had the entire gay-crisis. Thing is, I didn't—not really. I still found Beth and Sophie (the other volunteers)—one with a rack to die for and the other with the most perfect arse—extremely attractive. Heck, some nights I'd still pull out some old pictures of Kate I'd stored on my phone for a quick one off the wrist. But equally as often I'd imagine Ben in Kate's place, or me in Kate's place—with Ben in mine, if that makes any sense. I'd always known I wasn't gay, but I'd never realised I was this flexible. Like I said, Ben was a complication.

"Matthew." Ben had reached the edge of the pond.

I felt a jolt—I never knew that he knew my name. "Yeah. It's me." I struggled to my feet and wiped my raw palms against my trousers. "Sorry about this." I gestured at my sodden clothes, and realised I smelt slightly of mulch. Excellent impression, Matthew, well done. "I didn't mean to be a bother." I struggled out of the pond and back to the bank, plonking myself down on the grass.

"It all got a bit much, did it?"

I felt, rather than saw, Benjamin crouch down beside me.

"Sorry, don't mean to presume. I don't think we've been formally introduced. I'm Benjamin Smith—the painter." He put out his hand, ready to shake.

"I'd love to shake hands but..." I showed him my scuffed palms. "Matthew Merryweather." I smiled.

He bent over my hands, concerned, and I burst out laughing. "You've wrapped bunting around your hat!" I couldn't contain myself, it seemed both so perfectly in character, and so charmingly absurd. For someone I'd placed on a pedestal, a bedraggled blue flag poking down the collar of an almost white dress shirt was apparently just the thing to bring them down to Earth.

He looked up, under the brim of his hat, a soft smile—nothing like the electric one that usually lit up his face—playing around the corners of his mouth. "I may have bunting on my hat, young man, but you've the perfect name for a hobbit." He quirked his lips.

"At least my parents didn't name me Bilbo. Or Gandalf. Or Sauron. And I'm twenty-three!"

He broke out into a beaming smile, and I rocked back. The force of it, at such close quarters, was enough to make me feel just a little bit woozy. His smile vanished and he got to his feet. "Yes. Well, I'd better be off then. Now that I know you're all right."

"Stay." I said without thinking. I didn't mean to make it sound so desperate—or heartfelt. I hope to God he doesn't ask me why.

"Do you have some other injury?" His eyes catalogued my features. "You seem to be all right."

"No, nothing." I sighed. "It's just…" I leant forward, crossing my arms over my knees, and resting my head upon them. "It's fine. I'm fine. Go back to the party."

I heard him sit down again besides me. "I must say, I've found the party rather boring."

"Same old, same old."

He nodded.

"I guess I get why everyone is so happy, and I'm sure the monarchy are pleased to have someone to carry on the royal line, but sometimes I wonder…" I bit off my sentence there. I'd be a fool to continue.

"It's all so very staged." Ben said, pulling out tufts of grass. "The wedding, the coaches, the kisses. The only thing I found of any true meaning was the fly past by the Hurricane, the Spitfire, and the Lancaster Bomber—and even that was not truly about them. It brought back memories."

"Oh, come on." I turned to him, but his gaze was fixed somewhere in the middle of the pond. "Surely you're not old enough to remember the Second World War?"

His mouth quirked once more. "No, not that war." He picked a blade of grass, and began to chew on it. "It's just so futile, isn't it? War."

"My friends who went seemed to think it had a purpose." I thought a second and continued. "That being said, they were never really the same again."

"I suppose killing someone, or seeing someone killed, does that to you." He spat out the grass-stalk. "At least your friends came back." His face twisted for a second, like he might cry, and then returned to a mask of such normality that I wanted to reach out and smooth it back to its previous upset.

"Was it recent?" I could not stop myself from asking, and shifted towards him.

"No. Not Iraq, or Afghanistan. Bosnia, 1995."

"I remember that, sort of. I was seven. Some days, my parents wouldn't let me watch cartoons."

He laughed, hollowly. "I was twenty. Studying fine art at St Martin's in London. It was a wonderful, glorious time. University cushioned us from the recession, and I'd never thought that when I said goodbye it would be for the last time."

"I'm sorry." I didn't know what to say. "It was a close friend, I guess."

"We'd grown up together. He was my first friend at Harrow, and even though he'd managed to get himself into the army, I'd never expected him to go to war."

I reached out and placed my hand over his. "Really, I'm sorry."

"The worst part of it was, even though we'd grown up together, I never knew he knew, and I was always too scared to say anything." His eyes kept focus on the centre of the lake. "And then, I found out not only had he felt the same, but that he'd left me this." Ben pushed my hand aside, and gestured, all around us. "The stupid idiot left me this cottage and his inheritance. Even his stupid medals. But it's nothing. Really nothing. Comparatively."

A sick part of me twisted up in the joy of having an answer, but most of me was reeling in surprise. What on Earth prompted him to tell me...?

Ben smiled bitterly. "Oh, come on, Matthew Merryweather. You can't tell me you did not know. Everyone in the village knows about poor Benjamin Smith."

"I didn't. Honest. It's just—It's just I can't see why, knowing that you walk around with such a joyful smile." I blushed. "I'm sorry—I shouldn't have..." I got to my feet. "I'm sorry..."

"I smile because I'm here."

I stopped in my tracks.

"It could have been better, yes. But it could have been worse. He could have married and settled down with a wife and two perfect Harrovian children, gone into the city, grown a potbelly and a sanctimonious air. I could have lived my life, not knowing, always wondering. Instead, even though I was the basest form of coward, at least I know. And knowing and living are beautiful things."

"Oh. That's pretty deep."

"It's not really, Matthew. It is how it is."

I walked back and sat down. "No, I think it's pretty cool. I mean, that you can draw good things from it. That's good. I don't know if I'd have been able to do the same." Strangely enough, I meant every word I'd just said.

"I think you'd surprise yourself. I know, I certainly did."

"Though—living here. I guess it doesn't have the most vibrant scene?"

Ben turned and smiled at me, a proper, wicked 100watt smile. My knees trembled and I was very glad I was sitting down. "Why, Matthew. Are you interested?"

I felt myself blush, the warm-heat of the pinkness suffusing my face. "Maybe," I squeaked.

His mouth dropped open. "Oh. Um. Well." He flushed pink enough to match me. "I was under the impression from your mother that you had a girlfriend."

"Broke up with me via email." I shrugged. "Probably a good thing."

"I was also under the impression that you preferred women— I've seen you leering at Beth and Sophie when you're out having a fag…oh, bugger." Ben began to resemble a roast tomato.

"Ah, so you did notice me." It was too easy to tease him, though I figured much more and I'd have to call the first-aid guys over. "I'm only joking. Honestly, it's pretty much been women up until recently."

"And recently?" The words were like a whisper.

"Recently, I began to notice you." I leant forward, pushing

my chance, only to feel a firm hand push me back.

"Matthew, I'm not an experiment."

"I know. It's not because I'm bored, and you're a bloke, and I'm curious. It's just that you're you." I tried to smile. "I'm sorry, I shouldn't have presumed that you'd be interested."

"Interested is not at issue. There are more than ten years between us. I'm used to my own ways, my own life, my own house. I'd rather live in St Elena's than anywhere else. You're young, you need to learn about life."

I sniggered "Benjamin Smith—you might not be an experiment, but I'm also not naïve enough to presume I'm going to stay in St Elena's forever." I smiled, trying to will my sincerity into my eyes. "Look, I like you. Who knows what may happen in time? But right here, right now, I'd really not mind if we took a chance."

Ben smiled at me once more. "A chance. All right." He leant over and brushed his lips against mine. The bunting tickled my nose, and I couldn't help but laugh. Benjamin joined in, and soon we were rolling around in the grass, making the most of this much improved bank holiday.

Somehow, I don't see myself leaving St Elena's any time soon.

▲

About Chris Smith

CHRIS SMITH LURKS in the Home Counties with two cats and a very longsuffering husband. When not drawing buildings for cash, Chris Smith can be found glued to her computer. She has heard of "outside" and often ventures forth to investigate, though she is relatively sure that "sunshine" is a myth.

What Katy Did on Holiday
by Stevie Carroll

"I'M GOING TO have an adventure," Katy said. The assorted soft toys arrayed haphazardly on her shelves said nothing, but she suspected the majority disapproved. "A proper adventure," she clarified. "I've spent too long being boring."

So Katy packed her bags, jumped into her ageing pink Mini (with white Go Faster stripes), and set off in a north-easterly direction. She had a whole week until term started, all her lessons were planned—they had been since the first week of the summer holidays—and there were no plants to water or pets to feed. It was just her and her soft toys in their little flat. The toys could cope very well without her for a few days, in spite of the looks they'd continued to give her right up until she'd slammed the door on them, and begun her adventure.

When Katy first moved to Wales, living on her own and having her first proper grown-up job had been enough of an adventure by itself. Having survived the first term, though, she had realised she needed more. She needed a social life. Abergavenny wasn't much of a drive, but Katy didn't fancy walking into a pub by herself. The other teachers were older, married—to men—and already had friends and hobbies of their own. She'd thought about joining a sports team, but rugby made her nervous, and no one in Monmouthshire seemed interested in getting a netball team together.

So, for two terms, Katy had mostly stayed in and read. She had wallowed in school stories, mystery novels by Agatha Christie and her ilk, and picture books. She read those to her class too, of course, but sometimes it was nice to put her feet up with a glass of wine, and read the adventures of Mrs Murgatroyd and her giant rabbit just for fun.

Mrs M and Bunny had become popular recently, but Katy had been collecting the books since the very first one came out. The central characters travelled the British Isles, latterly in a distinctive VW camper van, befriending the locals and solving very small mysteries. Katy had slipped her three favourites—all a little dog-eared—into her suitcase. She would have been embarrassed to take a teddy on the adventure, but the books would comfort her in case things became more exciting than she anticipated.

Hay-on-Wye wasn't that far away. It was just over the border, near enough that she could walk back from England into Wales. Going to another country, even if it was, in fact, the country you had been born in, surely counted as an adventure. The Mini certainly thought so, being reluctant to reach speeds of over forty miles an hour the whole way. Katy tried to sympathise with it, patting its dashboard, or the centre of the steering wheel, in an encouraging way whenever they reached another hill. Once their adventure was over, she would send it away for a proper service. She might even see if someone could give it a new engine.

Hay certainly had a lot of bookshops! And pubs, come to think of it. Katy decided to stay at the big whitewashed hotel with cheery, well-kept hanging baskets all around its walls. It might not be the cheapest accommodation in town, but she'd saved a little this year, in spite of her student loan repayments.

After a tasty and hearty lunch, washed down with a pint of local beer, Katy set off to explore the bookshops. There were many, many more than she had counted on her drive into town, and she ran back to the hotel to hide two of her three credit cards under the Mrs Murgatroyd books in her suitcase. With only one credit card, and only one pair of hands to carry her purchases, she might just manage not to break the bank. Especially considering that her poor Mini would have to transport the books home, come the end of the week.

Outside bookshop number nine on her tour, Katy spotted a sandwich board listing upcoming book signings. Tomorrow morning the shop would be playing host to Elizabeth Harris, author of the Mrs Murgatroyd books! Heart pounding and head spinning, Katy took a step back, coming to rest against a window sill. She contemplated going home for her copies of the other books in the series. That would seem too enthusiastic. Heading into scary stalker territory. She would take along the three she had, and buy the new one if it was out. Asking to have four books signed wasn't crazed fan level, not when she could rightfully say that she was a primary school teacher.

▲

THE NEXT DAY dawned grey and drizzly. Undeterred, Katy pulled on a clean pair of jeans, a smart T-shirt, and newly polished low-heeled boots. The book signing started at ten, and she wanted to be as close to the front of the queue as she could be. She rushed her breakfast, then sprinted back upstairs for her books. The sun was shining through her bedroom window, but she didn't trust the clouds threatening to obscure it again. Carefully sliding her Mrs Murgatroyd books into a plain carrier bag from the previous day's shopping expedition, Katy grabbed her rolled up cagoule and rushed outside.

The queue had already started outside the bookshop. Harassed parents clutched the hands and arms of wriggling, bouncing children, who outnumbered them two, or more, to one. Katy slowed down, feeling momentarily out of place. She was a teacher. Her pupils would love to hear how she met the author of Mrs Murgatroyd, along with any extra little facts she managed to glean about the characters and their adventures. She brightened, and started to consider what question they would most like her to ask while her books were being signed.

Just before reaching the corner of the shop building, Katy saw a flash of green. She glanced down the side, and there was Mrs Murgatroyd's camper van. At least, there was a camper van very much like the one featured in Mrs Murgatroyd's last few adventures. The van was old, but well cared for, a shiny dark green. British Racing Green, and it had the same cheery yellow and pink flowers stencilled on the doors and sides. Mrs M's camper had a roof-rack; this one was a Dormobile.

As Katy watched, a walking stick emerged from the driver's door, followed by an elderly woman. That had to be Ms Harris, who wrote the Mrs Murgatroyd books. Katy wondered if it would be cheeky to rush over and express her admiration. It probably would, and she might be too tongue-tied to make much sense anyway. Best wait until it was her turn at the book signing.

A young woman with short, bright pink hair, rushed around from the camper's passenger side to help Ms Harris. Arm in arm they set off towards the back of the shop building.

Katy continued on her way, and joined the queue. Half of her mind was puzzling over why the older woman had seemed so familiar, when she didn't remember seeing any pictures of Ms Harris. Not on the books' back covers—Katy peeked inside her carrier bag to be certain—and not in any of the glossy magazines they spread out on the tables, cut up for collages, or that she flicked through in the dentist's waiting room.

The other half of her mind was marvelling at the younger woman's hair. Katy wished she could be brave enough to dye her hair, or even to hack it short. She twirled the end of her plait around her fingers, wondering how the two women were related. Not mother and daughter, and certainly not sisters. Could they be partners? The age gap between them seemed too large, but some women made May-December relationships work.

The queue started to move forwards. Glancing back, Katy saw that there were almost as many people behind her as in front. She needed to come up with a snappy question that was original—she didn't want to seem unimaginative—and that would bear repeated tellings to her pupils. The pictures. She would ask about the pictures. Her pupils always asked about them.

Inside the shop, Katy tried to see around the tall man—and his two energetic children—in front of her. The older woman sat at a table; the younger woman stood just behind her left shoulder. One of the children at the front of the queue must have asked a question. Smiling, the woman with the pink hair crouched down to answer.

Ms Harris finished writing in a book, picked it up, and handed it to the waiting woman before her. She looked up at the woman, and Katy glimpsed her face. Miss Jones! Her favourite teacher at secondary school. The one who had retired after Katy had sat her GCSEs. It had never occurred to Katy back then to ask what teachers did when they stopped being teachers, or even what they did when not at school. Now she had part of the answer. Unlike Katy, some teachers regularly went out and had adventures. And some teachers had friends—or girlfriends—with bright pink hair. Katy willed the queue to move forwards faster.

"Katy Parker!" Miss Jones recognised her the moment she reached the front of the queue. "What brings you here? What are you doing with yourself these days?"

"I'm a teacher." Katy was suddenly very proud of her career choice. "At a village primary school on the other side of Abergavenny. I fell in love with the area when you took us there on those class hiking trips, and I was so pleased when the chance came up to work there." She took the three books from their bag, and laid them out on the table.

"My pupils love your stories," she continued. "They like Mrs Murgatroyd and Bunny, but they also like looking at all the different people in the illustrations. Was it your idea to make the characters so diverse?" Not only did the scenes in the books feature characters of all ages and ethnicities, there were also people with disabilities, children with only one parent, children with two mothers or two fathers, children who lived with their grandparents. And so the list went on.

"I suppose I can take part of the credit," Miss Jones said. "Having worked in such a mixed school all those years, it seemed natural to include everyone in the stories. Most of the credit for the crowd scenes, though, belongs to Helena."

The woman with pink hair took a small step forward. She had silver studs all the way up one earlobe, and halfway up the other. Katy's hand darted to the labrys stud in her own ear, wondering whether Helena had spotted it, and recognised its significance. Feeling her cheeks heat up a little, Katy forced her hand back down to her side.

"My niece," Miss Jones continued. "I used to tell stories to all my nieces and nephews when they were growing up, but she was the one who encouraged me to write them down."

"You illustrate the stories?" Katy hoped she wasn't staring too obviously at Helena's pale skin, freckled cheeks and tiny button nose.

"I do," Helena said. "I work with several authors, and take on commissions for other projects, but Aunt Viv is my favourite person to draw for."

"And you really live in a camper van?"

"Not for much longer," Miss Jones said. "My knees can't take another winter." She indicated the people waiting behind Katy. "We're holding them up with our chatter. Do you want to meet us for dinner tonight? I always like to hear how my favourite pupils have been getting on since school."

⋏

WALKING BACK TO the hotel, her books clutched tightly to her chest, and with an extra spring in her step, Katy noticed the town in far greater detail than she had the previous day. Most of the houses and shops were grey stone with brightly painted doors and windows—like the one next to her hotel, with its cheerful blue details—but some were whitewashed like the hotel, and one or two buildings had black timber frames. Everywhere she saw colourful, well-tended window boxes and hanging baskets. Even without the dinner invitation to look forward to, she would always love Hay after her morning's adventure.

She stowed her books safely in her suitcase then, leaving her cagoule behind—the clouds had all but disappeared—she set off up the steep narrow footpath to the stone castle. It wasn't a castle as her pupils would picture one, although the ruined keep at the far end might appeal to them. Hit by a sudden inspiration, Katy bought a souvenir notebook and pencil from the bookshop at the opposite end, and tried to sketch her impressions of the castle and its visitors.

To her eyes the castle was made up of three parts: the ruined keep at one end, the ruined mansion house in the middle, and the intact portion of the house at the other end. Katy hoped that Mrs Murgatroyd's next excursion would be to Hay. Her own little sketches barely did any part of the castle justice, so it would be wonderful to see it depicted by a professional artist, and it seemed the perfect setting for an adventure with Bunny. Katy's pupils would want to know where 'Miss' had been for her holidays, and while taking photos on her phone was a help, paper seemed more permanent. Some of them would have been away for a week or more, and some would have been on days out, but almost half would have been at home in the village all summer. Katy couldn't take them on trips the way Miss Jones had taken her class on holiday, but she could bring faraway places to the class, through sketches, photographs and picture books.

The other visitors seemed more interested in browsing the books than in looking at the buildings or at the view down to the town. Watching them, Katy noticed a higher proportion of white people than in Helena's pictures, and not many people with obvious disabilities, although that might be because of the castle's location. Their accents were mostly Welsh, English and North American, with a few Scots and Irish mixed in.

Adding some stick people to her sketches, Katy wondered if Helena would draw her in a crowd scene one day. Helena had smiled when her aunt had suggested dinner. Katy resolved to offer them an open invitation to visit any time that they happened to be passing. Her landlord was so rarely at home; he could hardly object to Katy's friends parking a camper van on his drive for a day or so. Perhaps they'd get a car if they were settling down. Perhaps—Katy's heart sank—Helena would continue travelling on her own, and be unavailable to visit with her aunt.

Helena had seemed friendly on first impression, and Katy needed more friends—especially friends only a year or two older than her. Helena was pretty—in a slightly tomboyish way—and Katy missed having a girlfriend. Katy had worked so hard the past couple of years that she had barely had time to date, but now she was settled in her job, and her little flat. It was time she started looking again. Helena seemed like she'd make a fun girlfriend—and she'd certainly spent that little bit longer looking at Katy than would be expected if she wasn't interested.

Katy needed to make a good impression. She should show both women that she was a proper grown-up, but not afraid to have fun. Jeans and a T-shirt were acceptable for a book signing, but she should wear something smarter for dinner. They were dining in her hotel at Miss Jones'—at Vivienne's—suggestion, so she didn't need to worry about a coat. Just a smart pair of trousers and a blouse, and there had to be a charity shop somewhere amongst the book shops.

▲

LATER, KATY LOOKED at herself in the bathroom mirror. Her new outfit was showier than she had planned: satin trousers and a top that showed off more of her arms than she was used to, but she'd found a bargain, even with the matching shoes. She'd found time to file and paint her nails (a girly pink that she liked, although it didn't quite match her skin tone). In a flurry of optimism, she switched the labrys stud for a paired-Venus drop earring, and set off down to the restaurant. Some people might accuse her of being too obvious, but others—mostly her closest friends—had previously told Katy that she was too subtle for her own good.

Vivienne and Helena were waiting for her at the bar. Katy stifled a giggle as she realised that Helena had substituted one of her studs for an earring that matched Katy's. Maybe she hadn't been wrong after all. Helena wore a plain black T-shirt with embroidered jeans, and her aunt wore a smart skirt-suit. Katy wondered if she'd overdressed, although both women assured her that she looked splendid.

Over dinner Katy found herself quizzed about her life since school, about her current post, and about her mother.

"In Provence with her third husband." Katy turned to Helena, feeling a sudden need to explain. "My parents met at a festival the year they both finished their first year at university. They travelled together all summer, then went their separate ways before Mum realised about me." Katy reached for her water glass. "I don't think any of her subsequent men could cope with her having a successful career at the same time as raising a daughter." She took a drink. "Not that I think my real father would have been any better. I don't know much about him beyond his name and that both his parents were second generation British."

Katy set her glass back down. That answered all the obvious questions Helena might have, right down to the fact that Katy's colouring was slightly too brown to be a year-round suntan.

"And your new stepfather?" Vivienne asked.

"Not so new," Katy said. "So far he seems the best of the lot." She turned to Helena again. "How about you? Will you carry on travelling after your aunt settles down?"

"Not so much." Helena picked up the wine bottle and re-filled all their glasses. "I'm going to stay with Aunt Viv. Her new house has plenty of room for both of us, and I've got a part-time job at the museum to supplement my income from illustrating."

"Oh." Katy bit her lip. "You never said where you were moving to," she asked Vivienne. "Is it far from your other relatives?"

"I've bought a house in Abergavenny," Vivienne said. "I've always loved the area just as much as you obviously do."

Katy was stunned. She would have local friends next year. Friends who liked lots of the same things she liked, and who weren't work colleagues. She could see herself finding plenty of reasons to visit the museum if Helena was going to be working there.

▲

THE SUN WAS shining brightly the next morning, and Katy studied the leaflet detailing local hiking routes. She really ought to get out and about before returning home the next day. Getting away from the town would keep her from buying more books, when she was already concerned about how to fit those she had into the Mini. Also, she wouldn't be constantly wondering if Helena and Vivienne had left yet. They had other stops planned on this tour, before moving into their new home, and Vivienne had said that meant setting off before lunchtime.

They'd exchanged addresses and phone numbers, of course, but Katy knew how busy a new house and a new job would keep Helena right up until the end of the year. Maybe she should have been more vocal in her offers of help. If only she knew Abergavenny better, she could have offered to show Helena around once the house was in some kind of order. Assuming Helena's work didn't keep her too busy for socialising, that was.

There was a knock on the door.

Katy sprang to her feet, and looked around, guilty that she hadn't tidied before the hotel maid service arrived to clean.

There was another knock, which was odd, because maids usually let themselves in. Maybe this one had forgotten her keys.

Katy opened the door, and there was Helena. She wore white T-shirt, shorts and trainers; a sports bag was slung over one shoulder and a big orange ball was tucked under her other arm.

"Do you play basketball?" She looked Katy up and down. "You don't seem the type for rugby."

"I used to play netball."

"You'll soon pick it up, then. Got anything you can change into? I'll wait for you down at the playing field. It's about ten minutes' walk; I'm sure they'll give you directions if you ask at the reception desk."

▲

BASKETBALL WAS EASIER to play with just two people than netball would have been. While Helena was taller, and more used to moving with the ball, Katy found that being small made her better at dodging. Running around after primary school children wasn't the same as playing sports regularly, however, and she was soon out of breath. It didn't help either that she kept being distracted by the way Helena's breasts bounced inside her T-shirt, or by how strong her legs looked from the hem of her short white shorts right down to the tops of her white ankle socks.

"Having fun?" Helena dropped down next to Katy onto the bench she had finally been forced to retreat to. Running a hand through her hair, Helena pushed back the strands that had fallen into her face.

"I am." Katy turned to face Helena. "I think I can manage another game in a few minutes."

"I've found a team I'm going to join as soon as I'm settled

in," Helena said. "They're always looking for new players, if you want to come along too. I can put in a good word for you."

"I'd like that. Joining the team, I mean, and I'd be very grateful if you could introduce me." Katy turned away. "I'm not very good at meeting new people."

"You came here on your own, didn't you?" Helena reached out and turned Katy's head back towards her. "I'd never have plucked up the courage to come and find you before we left if Aunt Viv hadn't nagged me."

"You don't seem shy." Katy looked down at her hands. They felt clammy, even after she'd rubbed them against the fabric of her jeans.

"I'm not usually. You can't be with Aunt Viv around." Helena reached across to place her hands over Katy's. "But I'm settling down now. I have to think about what I do. If I were to kiss a woman today, we'd both be in the same county as each other next week, next month. Probably next year. It's not like I'll be living in a big city where it'd be easier to avoid my exes either."

"If you were to kiss a woman today…" Katy considered the matter carefully. "Do you want to kiss me?"

"Do you want me to?"

Katy wasn't in the habit of kissing women she'd only just met. Not since her first year at university, not while sober, and certainly not in the middle of a park during the school holidays. Then again, this was supposed to be Katy's big adventure before she went back to being sensible for the new term.

Katy turned to face Helena. Leaning forward, she kissed her quickly on the lips. Then she pulled away, and looked back down at their hands, which now seemed to be twined together.

Helena untangled one of her hands from Katy's and brought it slowly up to rest against Katy's cheek.

"I think we can do better than that." She slid her hand round to the back of Katy's neck and pulled her forward into a much longer kiss.

Katy's lips parted. Her tongue met Helena's. She shifted on

the bench until she was straddling Helena's lap. She followed the waistband of Helena's shorts with her hands until they met in the small of Helena's back.

A dog barked close by. Its bounding footfalls were getting closer.

Katy scrambled off Helena's lap. She could feel her cheeks heating up. The big, yellow dog had turned around, and was already bounding back to his owners.

"What's wrong?" Helena took hold of Katy's hands. "Don't you like having an audience?"

"I…" What if one of the children were to see her? Or their parents? Anyone she knew might have decided to come here on one last day-trip before term started. Over on the far side of the playing field, the dog was happily greeting its owners. "Can we just walk?"

"If you want." Helena checked her watch—a fancy sports one with lots of extra dials and digital displays. "I'll have to head back soon anyway. Aunt Viv will be wondering where I got to, and I should really find somewhere to have a shower before we hit the road. Who knows where we'll end up parked tonight?"

"You could use my bathroom at the hotel." Katy wasn't usually so forward, but then she *was* on an adventure.

"Don't mind if I do." Helena got to her feet, and extended a hand towards Katy. "Shall we go?"

▲

KATY FELT AS if she'd talked non-stop all the way back, but she couldn't have done, because Helena had been talking too. Helena wanted to draw her: not as a character in the crowd, but as someone Mrs Murgatroyd was going to help on one of her upcoming adventures. Helena had a big project at the museum—although very little funding—to draw new illustrations for displays that hadn't been updated in years. Helena knew where the best pubs, cafés and restaurants were in Abergavenny, although she hadn't visited them yet, and she wanted to take Katy with her.

They were back in the hotel, and up in Katy's room in no time.

Katy used the time while Helena was showering to make two cups of tea, and dig out her emergency packet of short-bread from her suitcase. There was only one chair in the room, so she pulled the little table from over by the window to by the bed, then sat there and waited.

Helena came back soon enough, still towelling her hair. She wore jeans so faded they were almost white, and a bright blue T-shirt that matched her eyes but clashed a little with her hair. Sitting on the bed next to Katy, she placed herself close enough that Katy could smell the hotel's shampoo and shower gel on her.

"Well," she said. "Here we are."

"Here we are," Katy repeated.

"And no barking dogs this time."

"No." Katy shook her head, partly for emphasis, but mostly because she was unsure how to proceed. She liked Helena. She liked her a lot. But they both wanted more than a holiday romance, and things were possibly moving too quickly when they might not see each other again for a month or more.

Helena reached out for the teacup. It rattled in its saucer, and a few drops of tea splashed out as she brought it up to her lips.

"I didn't know if you took milk." Katy indicated where the little cartons sat next to the sachets of sugar.

"I don't."

"Neither do I." Katy's teacup rattled even louder as she tried to lift it from its saucer. She put it back down again without drinking, and reached over to Helena, guiding her cup down to the table.

They looked at each other, Katy fighting the urge to giggle nervously, then giving up when she realised that Helena was too.

"A fine pair we make," Helena said when she finally stopped laughing. She pulled out a tissue and dabbed at her eyes. Then she turned it around, and dabbed at Katy's eyes with another corner. "You know, you really are pretty when you laugh."

"Doesn't my face go all crinkled up? Like this?" Katy tried to demonstrate.

"It certainly doesn't." Helena took hold of Katy's hands. Then she leaned forward, and kissed her.

They fell backwards onto the bed, somehow managing not to kick the table over as their legs tangled together. Helena's kisses made Katy feel giddy: as if she had stood at the very top of a hill and spun round and round until finally she fell over. Her head was between two piles of pillows. Helena was pressing her hands into the pillows, one on each side of her head. Katy gripped Helena's hands tightly as they kissed deeper and deeper.

A mobile phone chirruped.

"Was that you or me?" Helena sat up, straddling Katy's legs.

The phone chirruped again.

"That'll be mine then." Helena dug in the pocket of her jeans and pulled out a tiny, tiny phone, flipping it open as she did so. "Aunt Viv wants to know where I am. We should have left an hour ago." She closed the phone and stuffed it back into her pocket. "I'm sorry." She leaned forward to kiss Katy. "It'll have to be third time lucky." She got off the bed. "Call me. Text me. Email me. Let's arrange to meet up on the first of October. Tell me where as soon as you decide."

Katy nodded, too frustrated to speak. She glared at the door as it clicked shut behind Helena's pert bottom, then took a deep, calming breath. Maybe they were better taking things slowly. They had a month in which to get to know each other properly. They could send each other sexy emails, and have long, naughty phone conversations. Anticipation would make their reunion so much more enjoyable. This really had been a proper adventure—and Katy got the feeling it was the start of a much bigger one.

▲

About Stevie Carroll

BORN IN SHEFFIELD: England's Steel City, and raised in a village on the boundary of the White and Dark Peaks, STEVIE CARROLL was nourished by a diet of drama and science fiction from the BBC and ITV, and a diverse range of books, most notably Diane Wynne-Jones and The Women's Press, from the only library in the valley. After this came a university education in Scotland, while writing mostly non-fiction for various underground bisexual publications under various aliases, before creativity was stifled by a decade of day-jobs.

Now based in Hampshire, Stevie has rediscovered the joys of writing fiction, managing to combine thoughts of science fiction, fantasy and mysteries with a day-job in the pharmaceuticals industry and far too many voluntary posts working with young people, with animals and in local politics. Stevie's first published story, 'The Monitors' (in Noble Romance's *Echoes oOf Possibilities*), was long listed by the 2010 Tiptree Awards jury.

Stevie currently has multiple projects on the boil, including at least two novels, a novella and several short stories. Updates on all of these are currently to be found at Stevie's Livejournal, although a website is in the planning stages and will go live towards the end of the year if not before.

Livejournal: stevie-carroll.livejournal.com
Email: stevie.carroll@dormouse.myzen.co.uk

Riding with Hob
by Alex Beecroft

MARK'S FINGERS SLACKENED. The single slice of cheddar in his sandwich slithered out and plummeted to smear his trainer with a trail of Branston pickle. *If I'd known there were going to be morris dancers, I wouldn't have come.*

He stood across the road from Ely Cathedral, his goal for the day. He had travelled up from university in London to examine its paintings and buttresses for his essay on the perpendicular style in medieval art and architecture. The morning had dawned sunny, and the train had been empty, leaving him a table of his own on which to prop his book. He'd tried to think of the trip as a holiday, promising himself something quaint when he finished. There was a famous tea-shop down by the river he intended to patronise for a proper afternoon tea at four o'clock, with cucumber sandwiches and a three layer cake-stand piled high with buns.

So it wasn't as though he was immune to the charms of cosy, cottagey, *someone should tell them it's the 21st Century* English afternoons, but morris dancing was a step too far.

A small crowd of people had gathered on the pavement where he stood, just one small road away from the Cathedral's imposing entrance. Middle aged men in top-hats and ragged jackets. Middle aged women in milkmaid outfits. At least, in his skinny jeans and Green Day T-shirt he didn't look as though he belonged with them.

Truth was, though, he didn't belong with anyone. The thought ambushed him as craftily as his cheese slice had, slithering out of nowhere, painting him with regret. "We're sorry, mate," his friends had said, "but we already found a house for next term and we just can't find space for you."

It didn't really hurt. He looked at the dancers who blocked the road, their faces red with effort, their clogged feet beating out a complex rhythm on the pavement, hankies brilliant white arcs against the cloudless sky. It didn't hurt because he'd been expecting it. He was used to it. Other people would have taken friends on a trip like this. He came alone. He had not asked for company because, if he had, no-one would have said yes.

At least the milkmaid women with their ridiculous arches of flowers had a tribe to belong to. Maybe if he put on a ragged jacket and painted his face, these men would think he was one of them.

The dance finished. Over by the wall that lined the cathedral grounds, the next group peeled out of their huddle and allowed a few cars to pass before they took their places. A younger group than the others, their faces covered by masks and their outfits some fanciful confection: half-medieval, half-Tolkien. He could go now, push past them, duck into the cool shade of the cavernous stone portico, and get on with his work. But the musicians were already in the road, laughing with each other under their broad brimmed hats, tucking their fiddles under their chins, and something in him, cowardice or awe, meant he didn't quite dare to walk out under their shadow-masked gaze.

And then the music started.

This was no see-saw, bumptious, yokel tune. It began faint and wound itself beneath his clothes, raising goosebumps on his skin. It spread out and settled into his pores, seeping through his skin, making the beat of his heart part of its rhythm. It swallowed his defences as a snake engulfs an egg, and he wanted to put his headphones on, block it out, but it was too late. *I have nowhere to go home to. No money for a place of my own. No one in the world to care.*

It felt like a cry, and certainly one of the dancers seemed to have heard it. He was dancing around the edges of the pattern and wearing on his hips a polished black oval of material with the head and tail of a horse. This troupe wore no bells, and their footfalls made no noise. They wound and pranced through the eerie tune in utter silence, except that the horse's jaw snapped sometimes with a sound like scissors snipping.

Now that jaw came towards Mark, rearing, bucking like a real horse, giving out a wild hot scent of sweat and straw. He thought he saw life in its eyes and flinched back, heart a-thunder.

"All alone?" The dancer circled him. Glimpses of Faberge hair, laughter under the green tendrils of mask, and something better in the eyes—interest, focused and fascinated, directed at Mark. Mark blushed as though he'd been flayed, felt it too— exposed, judged, found precious. *Wanted.*

"Nothing to lose?" the dancer asked.

There had been pavement under his feet, hadn't there? A road to cross? Mark looked now and it was meadow-land, the colour of champagne. Cornflowers, as brilliant blue as the dancer's eyes, swept up to the cathedral gates, but the portico itself was barred with a rusty portcullis.

"I'm seeing things."

"Yes." Now the dancers' feet crushed the grasses. Now the man in front of him sat astride a real horse, black as tar. "True things."

He reached down a hand. "I will make you laugh. I will show you every delight under the moon. Come with me."

"Why?" Mark tried as hard as he could not to believe this, but it was happening. If he pinched himself, yes, it bloody hurt. But nothing else did. Where a lifetime's rejection should have been, something new was bubbling up—effervescent, reckless, full of joy. Why *should* he be miserable if he could have this instead?

"Why not?"

He took a last glance. Faint shadows of cars and pedestrians passed ghostlike through the dancers, but the music was louder here and all the masks were dropped. A far horizon dazzled his eye with light, and his horseman looked down at him with wonder.

And yes, why not? Mark took the hand, jumped up. He didn't look back.

▲

About Alex Beecroft

ALEX BEECROFT WAS born in Northern Ireland during the Troubles and grew up in the wild countryside of the Peak District. She studied English and Philosophy before accepting employment with the Crown Court where she worked for a number of years. Now a stay-at-home mum and full time author, Alex lives with her husband and two daughters in a little village near Cambridge and tries to avoid being mistaken for a tourist.

Alex is only intermittently present in the real world. She has led a Saxon shield wall into battle, toiled as a Georgian kitchen maid, and recently taken up an 800 year old form of English folk dance, but she still hasn't learned to operate a mobile phone.

Website: alexbeecroft.com
Facebook: facebook.com/pages/Alex-Beecroft/67928469701
Twitter: @Alex_Beecroft

Bloody Mathematicians
by Charlie Cochrane

AS THE OFFICIAL biographer of Stewart and Coppersmith, Charlie Cochrane is sometimes asked whether the lads ever had a severe falling out. They did, although the matter has only recently come to light, having been recorded among some confidential papers which were temporarily lost to the nation when Jonty Stewart stuck them down the back of a sofa.

The rest of their adventures can be found in the *Cambridge Fellows Mystery* Series.

▲

Cambridge 1909

"BLOODY MATHEMATICIANS." JONTY Stewart threw a sheaf of papers onto the desk and shook his head, sending his shock of blond hair flying and looking more than ever like a great, angry, tawny cat. "As far as I'm concerned the Vice-Chancellor should take a gun and shoot the lot of them."

"Wouldn't it be better if he took all their slide rules and stuck them up their…" Luckily, Dr Panesar's remark was never finished. Mrs Ward, the lady who usually kept Doctors Stewart and Coppersmith supplied with tea and cakes, knocked on the door and produced a brew intended to sweeten the tempers of the men who drank it. Not that there was much chance of it working in Jonty's case. Once the door was closed, and half a cup consumed, Panesar was brave enough to carry on. "What have they done now? And is it all of them or just one or two? A fraction, as 'twere?" He laughed at his joke, which was the only sign of matters carrying on as normal in this corner of Cambridge.

Jonty grimaced "I think the problem lies with the whole boiling. They came out of their mothers' wombs spouting calculus and taking no notice of anything else unless it had a power or an integral or something equally dire. But this time it's one in particular. The usual one." He sipped his tea, bit off a huge chunk of Eccles cake and sighed.

"Dr Coppersmith?" It had become a running topic of conversation, the sudden antagonism between the two St Bride's dons who'd once been inseparable. It was fortunate Orlando had moved back into college before blows had been struck. They'd once been friends, great friends some said—perhaps *more than friends* one or two surmised, to have reached such a fever pitch of antipathy—although nobody had any idea what had caused such a bitter estrangement. Perhaps the two men didn't even really know for themselves.

"The very chap." Jonty frowned, drained his tea and shook his head. "This time it was all a matter of where I parked my bicycle. I'd been visiting someone at St Bride's and apparently where I'd chosen to leave my conveyance is where he seems to think he has divine right to leave his. There was very nearly a punch up."

Panesar sniffed; he still had a lot of time for Coppersmith, even if Jonty seemed to be developing hatred for the whole mathematical breed. Mind you, there were times when the object of his anger could be absolutely insufferable, especially when he was sure he was in the right. "What stopped you having fisticuffs this time?"

"Summerbee from the porters' lodge, who offered to move

my bike to a much nicer and more salubrious place. Dr Copper-smith couldn't be his usual officious self in front of the man." Jonty pushed his cup away. "Or perhaps it's only me he seeks to be so abrasive with. I've heard people say he can still be a gentleman. He once was to me, but that's all in the past now. Water under the bridge."

"Do you think you'll ever reach a rapprochement?"

Jonty rose from his desk, shuffled his papers into order and shoved them under his arm. "Not now. I'd rather lead apes into hell like Beatrice than become friends with that man once more. I must have been mad..."

"I'll let myself out." Panesar closed the study door behind him but it didn't drown out the sound of Jonty muttering. He went out into the front garden of Forsythia Cottage then stood deep in thought, contemplating a little robin which was disporting itself in the dust. Something had to be done, and soon.

Dr Panesar suddenly grinned, cutting a little caper on the path. *Miss Peters, the Master's sister.* Of course. He must go down to St Bride's and rouse her out; Miss Peters would have a plan.

▲

ORLANDO COPPERSMITH MADE his way down Kings Parade, stopping to admire his visage in the window of Ryder and Amies. He liked the appearance of his newly grown beard and moustache; it made him look like one of King Arthur's more desperate knights, something which was out of keeping with his character although pleasing to his ego. He swaggered along to the tea shop where the Master of St Bride's was waiting for him, hopefully with the hot chocolate and rum babas ready for consumption.

"Coppersmith!" Dr Peters rose and greeted his colleague. "Been getting into arguments again? I could hear the row all the way to the Lodge."

Orlando rolled his eyes. "I apologise profusely. It was that bl...Dr Stewart again. Parking his bike where no decent man should. They drive you mad."

"People who park their bikes inconsiderately?"

"No. People who teach English. Dilettantes, the lot of them."

Peters smiled. "That seems a little harsh. They may spend half a lifetime wondering about one particular word in Hamlet but that's no reason to tar them all with the same brush."

"It's not just that. Take the way they dress. They look like..." Orlando stopped himself from saying "An army of Oscar Wildes coming down through the market". That would smack of protesting too much. "A load of scarecrows. It shouldn't be allowed."

Peters seemed like he was about to say something, then stopped himself, settling for looking out of the window at some young idiot from *the college next door* haring about on a bike. It was a good two minutes before he broke the silence. "You and Dr Stewart were such good friends."

Orlando took an even longer while to answer. "We were, as close as two men could be. But that was before..." Before what, exactly? They'd quarrelled—he couldn't even remember the cause now—and said the most stupid things. He'd packed a bag and left, the words "Good riddance!" sounding in his ears. "But that was before he settled for velvet jackets and ridiculous shirts." The excuse served as a place holder for what couldn't be said. "Now, on to more important things. What do you think of the new crop of freshers?"

Conversation turned to the merits, or lack of, among the first year students, the men chatting amiably—without a single mention of Dr Stewart—until it was time to move on to their next appointments. Orlando stepped out of the café, turned left and was proceeding in the general direction of St Bride's when he heard his name being spoken.

His mother had always warned him that people who eavesdrop never hear good of themselves, so he should have resisted the temptation. But he couldn't resist, especially when he recognised Miss Peters's voice. While he couldn't make out all that was said, the conversation in question taking place down a little side alley, he clearly heard, "Dr Stewart still thinks the world of Coppersmith, that's the sad thing. He wouldn't dare tell him so, of course, not after a fortnight pretending he hates the man."

And then someone who sounded remarkably like Lumley, the college chaplain, replied, "He hates that new beard and moustache, though. Anybody would wonder whether they're the reason Dr Stewart can't show his true feelings."

Orlando stormed back to St Bride's, eating up the ground with long strides and all the time muttering that it was beyond all decency for a dilettante to take umbrage at his moustache. He definitely didn't stop and look in the barber's window to see if the shop would be open early the next day.

▲

JONTY WAS PREPARING to cross St Bride's Old Court, to take a little snifter in the Senior Common Room before hall. He and Orlando had, during one of their earliest post-separation arguments, thrashed out the matter of who could frequent the SCR on which days, so any possible antagonism or embarrassment over the use of the chairs—*their* chairs, that once sacred and now accursed place where they first met—would be avoided.

He was passing one of the stairwells when Dr Panesar's voice caught his attention. Jonty would have normally walked straight on, his mama having warned him of the evils of eavesdropping, but the words overheard brought him up with a round turn.

"But that's the whole point. Dr Coppersmith doesn't hate Dr Stewart, far from it. I should know—I have to share the Common Room with him when the day of the month's even."

"Then why all this pretence and antagonism?" A deep female voice—Miss Peters's—answered. "Hardly a day goes by when they're not at blows, verbal or physical, and if they're not getting directly at each other then they're making snide little remarks to other people."

"Stuff and nonsense! All my eye and Betty Martin. They're just both too proud to say they'd actually like to make up and be pals again. Dr Coppersmith positively longs for that day, I can tell you."

When he eventually got to the SCR, after making a long detour around all of the college courts three times, Dr Stewart eschewed his usual pre-prandial small dry sherry in favour of a stiff whisky and soda. Which amazed everyone, not least himself.

▲

THE TOUCHLINE FOR the Cuppers match between St Bride's and St Francis's—two of the most fervent rivals in the university—was packed with both undergraduates and senior members of the colleges. Very few of them were mixing, eyeing each other up warily instead.

Orlando was wrapped up against the elements, ridiculously so, the large scarf swathing the lower part of his face definitely overdoing it given that the late autumn day was relatively mild. Some of the more hardy spectators were even sporting jackets as opposed to overcoats.

"Coppersmith!" Panesar came over and slapped Orlando's shoulder. "You're trussed up like a chicken, man. Are you coming down with something?"

"Hmphmughm."

"Sorry? I can't hear a word you're saying." Panesar reached over and grabbed the end of the scarf. "Take this thing off, for goodness sake."

Orlando began to swat his colleague's hands away but couldn't overcome him. Panesar had once been a handy boxer who more than punched his weight and Orlando was no match for him.

"Well, I'm jiggered." Panesar grinned. "Now I know why you were wearing this. Miss Peters, come and look at the show. Old Father Time's lost his whiskers."

Orlando snatched the scarf but didn't try to put it back on. He had no need any more; the cat was well and truly out of the bag.

"When did that come off then?" Miss Peters had come across and was now circling Orlando as if he was a statue worth close inspection.

"When I got fed up with it. A man can't wear whiskers all his life."

"Old Grace at *the college next door* does. His beard almost reaches his waist. They say he started growing it when he went into long trousers." Miss Peters laughed.

"Anyone who goes to *the college next door* can't be regarded as anything but a law unto himself. What they do doesn't apply to decent human beings." Orlando snorted. "Anyway, I decided I would put away childish things and therefore I'm close shaven again."

"And it suits you." A clear, well spoken voice came from over Panesar's shoulder and the group broke up to reveal Jonty, smiling shyly and evidently making an assessment of the beardless wonder in front of him.

"Thank you." Orlando could hardly get the words out, not because of a need to shout at the man, a need he'd experienced every moment of this past fortnight, but because he suddenly felt bashful and embarrassed.

"There's one of my students. Let's go and ask him difficult questions about electrons." Panesar drew Miss Peters away, leaving the two reticent fellows to converse in peace.

"I never thought you'd get rid of that thing. It made you look a bit raffish, you know. Quite out of character." Jonty smiled again, blue eyes dancing with what seemed like tentative delight.

A week previously Orlando might have answered, "How do you know anything about my character? Keep your opinions to yourself, sir." But now he just blushed and said, "I'd come to that conclusion myself." There was an awkward pause. "You look well."

"I feel well. Had a nasty cold last week that seemed to want to go on my chest, but otherwise…" Jonty wasn't allowed to continue.

"Are you sure you're well enough to be out?" Memories of Jonty lying at death's door with the flu came back to haunt Orlando. "Maybe you'd like to borrow…" He proffered the scarf, receiving another glorious smile in return.

"No need for that. I'm well padded. I should go and join the rest of the English lads now—I don't want to be labelled a renegade for associating with mathematicians. Perhaps we could have a pint after the game or whenever…"

"I should like that very much. Thank you." Orlando shook hands to mark the first hesitant step on the road to a possible rapprochement.

▲

JONTY STEWART SAT in his favourite chair in the lounge at Forsythia Cottage, watching the flames of the fire and imagining dragons as he had when a boy. He had a dark, handsome head on his knee and was gently stroking the curls adorning it. Orlando's suitcases were in the hall, waiting to be unpacked, and a delightful supper—all the runaway's favourite foods—was inside their tummies.

"Why did it take so long? For a rapprochement, I mean." Jonty sighed. "Two whole weeks. We must have been mad."

The owner of the head shook it. "Not mad in my case. Just confused. As usual." Orlando looked up, a rueful smile flickering on his lips. "It all went so fast, you see. I'd assumed we were set for the great happy ever after and the next minute we were at each other's throats. I supposed it was all up. I know it was the coward's way to just up and leave, but it was the only thing I could do. And then I had to persuade myself that I didn't like you so I wouldn't mope around all the time wanting what I could no longer have."

"You daft thing. You should hear Mama and Papa when

they start going hammer and tongs. Always gets made up with a kiss, though." Jonty kissed his Orlando's brow, just to illustrate the point. "It's what people deeply in love do, at times."

"My parents used to row. I'm not sure they were in love, though." Orlando snuggled his head against Jonty's thigh. "Glad we've made up."

"So am I." Jonty stroked his friend's head again. "Although I have to ask, what changed your mind? Why the sudden razing of the whiskers and the proffering of the hand of friendship?"

Orlando's mathematical brain had already registered the lack of logic in everything which had happened the last two days, but in regard to Jonty his logic had always disappeared. "I heard Miss Peters and Lumley talking yesterday. They said that you..." he avoided saying *thought the world of me* as it smacked of vanity, "still liked me and had only been pretending to be cross. That you couldn't reveal your feelings because of the fungus." He stroked his face.

"The swines!" Jonty slapped his knee, just avoiding Orlando's ear. "The sneaky little...I overheard Miss Peters and Dr Panesar nattering last evening before hall. They said you didn't hate me really, but were too proud to make up again. We've been had, good and proper." He began to laugh.

"Of all the..." Orlando laughed too, both of them descending into a fit of the giggles unbecoming for fellows of a noted Cambridge college. And, given what the next activity they were going to indulge in was likely to be, that would also be regarded as being unsuitable for senior members of that august body. Kissing of any sort was frowned upon within the walls of St Bride's, as were fond caresses and tender murmurs of love and affection. Downright sodomy should have shaken it to its very foundations. But it hadn't in the past, and while the occasions Jonty and Orlando actually "did their duty" within the hallowed environs were now rare in the extreme, the walls still stood.

Small studies with hard, draughty floors were hardly conducive to it, anyway. Much better a nice big warm double bed in a private cottage far away from St Bride's.

"Come on." Jonty tipped his head towards the door that led to the hallway. "Bed's waiting. Been too cold and lonely in there these last two weeks."

"You should try going back to a college bed for a fortnight. Hard as iron." Orlando got up, pulling Jonty with him. "I used to lie awake and think of you and curse myself for being an idiot."

"Being an idiot's what you're best at." Jonty gave his lover a kiss and they took the rest of the journey in silence, touches to hands, elbows, the small of the back, saying all that was needed. When they reached Orlando's room, turning right at the top of the stairs—as opposed to left for Jonty's—by unspoken mutual consent, they slammed the door to, shutting out the rest of the world and the stupidity of a fortnight before.

"Have you been sleeping here?" Orlando didn't need to ask the question; the signs of occupation would have been evident to the dullest of wits.

"Of course." Jonty strode over to the window, drawing the curtains closed. "At first to comfort me and then as a sort of call for you to come back. When you didn't, I stayed on—thought it might punish you."

"Now who's the idiot?" Orlando made a lunge for his lover but Jonty pounced, pushing him over onto the bed, suit, boots and all, and pinning him down. Orlando may have been the taller by a good few inches but his wiry frame couldn't compete with Jonty's compact strength.

"Right, now that you're where you should be again, I want you to solemnly swear there'll be no more of this nonsense." Jonty's face was inches away from his friend's and, although he smiled, he was in deadly earnest.

"No more arguing?"

"That would be too much to ask. Of course we'll argue, we love each other too much not to." Jonty rubbed his forehead against Orlando's. "Just don't come over all melodramatic and flounce off."

"I didn't flounce, I..." Orlando stopped himself short. An argument now would be disastrous. Instead, he settled for a long, succulent kiss, which was always the most effective way to shut Jonty up and get him to loosen his grip. It usually made him loosen other things, too. Predominantly buttons, which soon began being tugged and pulled at.

Orlando broke from his lover's embrace to make a start at his own shoelaces, those treacherous, cantankerous things which knotted and twisted and wouldn't be tamed. Especially when his nerves were in such a peak of excitement and Jonty was nibbling on his ear. "Do leave off a moment or I'll never get these things off."

"Leave them on, then." Jonty had loosened Orlando's collar sufficiently to get his tongue working along the man's neck and onto his shoulder.

"If my shoes stay on I'll never get my trousers off." Orlando's fingers were now incapable of making any sort of controlled movement.

"Leave those on, too. This is no time for niceties and faffing about." It clearly wasn't, not given the excited state Jonty was in. "Time for 'quick's the word and sharp's the action'." Very quick and very sharp or Jonty's gun would be prematurely discharging.

"But how...?" They'd never before made love without the bottom half being disrobed; the logistics seemed daunting, if not impossible. And actually quite exciting.

"We'll work it out. Now do shut up. It's getting urgent." Jonty quietened his friend with a huge kiss, pulling him backwards onto the bed, and pushing his hips out, ready to receive him. "Would it be terrible to ask you to take me, right now?"

"Terrible? It's the best thing you've said in a long time." Orlando gave up worrying about the mechanics and sprang into action. The matter of the trousers half way down his calves would sort itself out if he just concentrated on reaching his intended target.

"Oh, I've missed this so much." Jonty spoke into his lover's hair.

"So have I," Orlando just managed to say before he lost the power of speech.

▲

"ORLANDO," JONTY LAY in the crook of his lover's arm, thinking about his beloved Shakespeare, as he often did at, or after, moments of high passion. "This whole saga's reminded me of something. You wouldn't ever want me to kill anyone, would you?"

Orlando pulled back, looking Jonty in the eye. "What an extraordinary question. I don't believe so, why?"

"I was just wondering whether you knew anyone called Claudio. Or maybe Claude."

"Not that I'm aware of."

"Oh, then don't worry." Jonty snuggled down again. "Much ado about nothing."

▲

About Charlie Cochrane

AS CHARLIE COCHRANE couldn't be trusted to do any of her jobs of choice—like managing a rugby team—she writes. Her usual genre is historical gay fiction, with increasing forays into the modern day. Her Cambridge Fellows series of Edwardian romantic mysteries were instrumental in seeing her named Speak Its Name Author of the Year 2009. She's a member of both the Romantic Novelists' Association and International Thriller Writers Inc.

Drop her a line at cochrane.charlie2@googlemail.com to sign up for her fortnightly newsletter or find her at one of her haunts:

Website: charliecochrane.co.uk
Livejournal: charliecochrane.livejournal.com
GLBT Wiki: bookworld.editme.com/CharlieCochrane
Twitter: @charliecochrane
Facebook: facebook.com/profile.php?id=100000878813798

We'll always have Brighton #2
by Zahra Owens

AUTHOR'S NOTE: This is a companion piece to a story in the free *British Flash* anthology, but can be read as a standalone.

▲

WHEN I LOOK out of the window I see the water dripping off the pavilion in front of our hotel room. The pebbles on the beach are wet as well, not from the rowdy sea, but from the rain that has been beating down on us for most of the afternoon. I see people scrambling around, hidden under umbrellas and huddled into raincoats, their feet stuck in wellies.

"Come back to bed."

I look over my shoulder and see you lying there, totally enveloped in no-longer-crisp white hotel sheets and thick blankets. Your light blond hair sticks out in all directions and your eyes are still closed but I can tell you're awake. Kind of. It hits me again how well I know you and how utterly familiar this all feels. It's hard to believe it's been four months since I've seen you like this.

"It's still raining," I say, returning my gaze to a man with a small child outside.

"All the more reason to get back under the covers." You

sound sulky and if this had been four months ago, I would have jumped at the chance, but now I'm more hesitant.

Yes, we made love again. For the first time in four months. We also used condoms again for the first time in almost five years. It was a dual feeling, familiar yet strange. I yearned, longed, ached for you while we were apart and now we're back together, I know we will have a long way to go before we'll be a couple again. I can only hope we'll make it. This is just the first step. A first step toward forgiveness and maybe, if I dare to hope, a first step toward the rest of our lives.

I pull myself away from the window, letting the curtains fall closed again, and slowly walk to the bed. As I sit down on it, your hand reaches out and I take it with some trepidation.

"You're cold."

I smile nervously when you still refuse to open your eyes. "It's cold outside and not too warm in here either."

"So get into bed?"

For the first time since we woke from our nap I see your blue eyes as you pull back the sheet and blankets. I get an unobstructed view of your slender, naked, boyish body and you're smiling invitingly.

"I'll make you cold too."

You pull on the hand you're still holding and shake your head. I have to let go to allow my borrowed hotel bathrobe to slide off my shoulders and then I crawl under the covers. It's a vain attempt to not let my icy skin touch your undoubtedly heated body until I've warmed up, but you slide against me and snuggle closer like you always used to do before. You push me down and kiss me relentlessly. You're always the domineering one when we're together and I let you gladly. I'm older than you and almost a head taller, and you are exactly the body type I always go for, but most of them are consummate bottoms. Only you are different and I love every minute of it. Now even more than ever.

You grind against me and you're hard, so out of habit I

start turning around as soon as we stop kissing. My erection digs into the slightly starched sheets and as you rub up against me, we easily slide into our particular rhythm. I'm still a little sore from earlier, but I don't care. I'm ready to feel you inside me again. I still yearn for you to confirm our first time wasn't a fluke. After a few moments you stop moving, though, and I become apprehensive.

"What's wrong?" I dare to ask after a few long moments of nervous silence.

You push your face against the back of my neck and inhale deliberately. "I missed the way you smell."

I like your heaviness, the way you feel when you're lying on top of me. You're not heavy by any means. You still look more boyish than manly and could undoubtedly pass for a fourteen-year-old although you're almost thirty. You don't act like a teenager, though, in or out of bed. You were always 'my man', never 'my boyfriend', not even when we first got together.

"I missed the way your skin tastes," you continue as if it's one long stream-of-consciousness and not interspersed with silences. I can feel your lips against my neck, and then your tongue. "I missed the way you feel." The stubble on your chin rasps against the sensitive skin between my shoulder blades. I don't dare move, afraid you'll stop the tender caresses and bring me back down to earth. I can't have that. I want to stay here forever, in our sheltered little cocoon, far away from the real world.

You don't up the ante, don't deepen our interaction and eventually you roll off me. When I turn my head to look at you, you're scrutinising me with the most tender expression on your face. You don't speak and I'm starting to brace myself for rejection. Instead, the smallest of smiles invades your face.

"You're going to end up with that line permanently etched into your forehead, you know," you say with mischief in your eyes. Your hand peeks out from under the covers and tenderly caresses it. I try to relax, but I can't.

It occurs to me that this is all a little strange.

Four months ago I was unfaithful to you and wracked by guilt, confessed my indiscretion. You blew your top, using expletives that would have made a sailor blush, and I ran. I ran from you and from the confrontation and from my own shame and moved out of our home that very same day. What had I expected to happen? We were exclusive and happy to be, yet I had succumbed to temptation. Then last week I called you. No, I was not welcome at your father's funeral, but yes, you were willing to meet me to talk, after everything was over. You suggested our favourite spot. Brighton, the pavilion across from the hotel we always stayed at during Pride week. I saw you standing there, jiggling from one foot to the other in a futile attempt to stay warm in your ever season-inappropriate attire. For once in my life I was on time, but you wouldn't have known, since it took me a good fifteen minutes to get up the nerve to approach you.

You were freezing and so you took me to your room and we tumbled into bed. It was like nothing had happened and we'd just been apart for a few days because of a business trip or a separate holiday.

"You think too much."

I look at you and realize I was probably miles away. You give me that look you always give me when I zone out and your infinite patience strikes me again. I know we need to talk; you deserve that much. But just like four months ago, I'd rather run. I hate the confrontation. It makes my heart race and my skin crawl.

▲

WHEN WE CAME up this morning, it took you forever to get warm. You'd been outside, waiting for me by the pavilion. This is our pavilion; the one we both ran into one glorious, and just as rain-soaked, afternoon almost seven years ago. It was lust at first sight, and I just happened to be the happy occupant of this very same hotel room then. Needless to say we didn't leave it much for the next two days and after going home to our own flats and realizing we were miserable without each other, we soon decided to combat the shortage of affordable housing in London by moving in together.

For six blissful years we shared everything. I'd never loved anyone the way I loved you and you didn't leave any doubts that you loved me too, so it was pretty perfect all around. Despite all this I managed to ruin everything within the space of a week.

A new colleague at work had started a spark in me. You and I had been in a rut for a while, spending too much time working and not enough quality time together, but I don't want to use that as an excuse. No matter the reason, I was the one who cheated and although neither of us could ever be called a saint—we are men after all—we'd early on agreed that we wouldn't have sex with other people.

I broke that rule.

▲

I GET UP out of bed. "I can't think straight when we're naked together," I state by way of apology.

"Okay," you say and I can't dismiss the disappointment in your voice. "Let's go out, to a place where we can talk without...distractions."

We get dressed and leave the room. It's still raining so we can't go far and you point at our little pavilion, so we make a dash for it and arrive reasonably dry.

At first we can't get started. I realise how much I always rely on you making the first move so now I'm also waiting for you to break the ice. You take forever. At least that's what it feels like.

"I won't deny it hurt. In fact I don't think anything ever hurt more. Not even being called to my dad's deathbed." You're standing with your hands on the railing, staring out over the sea as you tell me this. I want to take your hand to comfort you, but it feels out of place somehow.

"I'm sorry I wasn't there for you," I say instead. You nod without looking at me. "It's not that I didn't want you there, but Mum was really upset about us breaking up and I didn't want her to be reminded of that. It outweighed you wanting to say goodbye to him. I know you were close to Dad."

"I wanted to be there to support *you*."

This time you look at me and I see the hurt still fresh in your face. Now I want to pull you into my arms and give you the comfort I wanted to give you at the funeral, but I settle for taking your hand.

"I still love you. Because of what you did I realised I'd forgive you anything and still love you no matter what."

I smile as your words relax me. "That's not healthy, starling," I say, using the nickname I always used to use.

"I know," you admit. "I wasn't happy with it either when I realised how I felt, but it is what it is. I need you in my life."

"I'll never do it again." I realise I sound like I'm begging, but I'm past feeling ashamed of it. You opened yourself up to me, so it's only fair I do the same.

"Don't say that. Temptation is everywhere."

"I resisted for six years and it wasn't even that hard. All I had to do was think of you and I knew it wouldn't be worth it, no matter how gorgeous he was. He'd never be as perfect as you."

You pull your hand away and resume your staring over the water. I try not to take it personally but I do worry about what I said wrong.

"I'm not perfect. You of all people should know that. You're not perfect either and I like it that way. I like the little imperfections in people. I like that you work too hard. And I also like that at work you're fine making decisions all day, but at home, when it's just the two of us, you couldn't make a decision to save your life. It's frustrating at times, but it's you. I know where I stand with you."

I move my hand on the railing so our little fingers touch and you lift your finger so it grabs mine. It's one of those little things we used to do when we were in public and couldn't show affection, like around my parents.

"I wish my parents were more like yours," I say.

You look at me as if you want to tell me I'm daft, but you don't say anything and I realise you can't read my thoughts. "I was thinking this was what we always used to do around my parents." I look at our entwined little fingers. "Because they can't stand us showing affection." I smile as another memory invades my mind. "That first time you took me to meet your parents, your dad invited me into the library and I was scared he was going to tell me to stay away from you. Instead he welcomed me into the family and told me that he didn't know 'how us boys acted around each other' but that he and his wife liked to show they loved each other in public and that he wouldn't have a problem with you and me doing the same."

You look at me in wonder. "I never knew that."

"That's why he was so special to me, your dad."

I see your eyes fill with tears and before I can react you grab me around the waist and squeeze me so all I can do is envelop you in my arms and rock you. You pull back and unbutton my sheepskin coat, which I know you only like because it's so warm, and push your arms underneath it. You're a runt so I can almost pull the coat all the way around you.

"Please come back to me?" you murmur against my neck, and all I can do is nod.

You don't let go of me as we walk back to the hotel room and this time when we undress and crawl back into bed, the lovemaking is so much more about getting reacquainted than it is about quelling our lust. This time, as you caress and lick my skin, it doesn't feel desperate, like it's our last time. This time it feels like we're starting again.

We make love face-to face, something we only used to do when we took the time, on lazy Sunday afternoons of which we'd had way too few the months before our breakup. I make a mental note to plan more of those, but then your mouth on me distracts me. I want to reciprocate, but you shake your head and continue to suck me off. You know exactly what to do to make me soar and as I groan in frustration, your hand reaches up for me and you give me your fingers to suck on. It's not enough, obviously, but then I taste you and I know you've been touching yourself, and this makes the heat rise at such an alarming rate that I can't stop myself from coming. As I lie in the aftermath, totally unable to move, you slide yourself next to me and I don't even have to open my eyes to imagine the self-satisfied grin you always wear when you made me lose it. I run my hand over your smooth back, remembering how good you always felt and still do, and I know I never want to compromise that again.

"I love you," I whisper and I hope it's loud enough for you to hear. I don't dare to open my eyes just yet, in case your reaction isn't what I expect. You move higher up and your mouth caresses my eyelids, so I open them.

"Marry me," you say.

I'm startled and try to gauge whether you're serious. We had this discussion when civil ceremonies became legal and then your views were clear. You wanted a full marriage, not just the "gay version" and you wanted to wait, hoping you could call me your husband sometime in the near future.

"It's not called a marriage, remember?"

You nod. "I don't care. I want to tell the world we belong together. Forever. We hit a speed bump, that's all. I want to put a ring on your finger."

"I don't need a reminder. I just wish your dad could have been here to see this."

"I'm glad he's not around to see what I'm going to do to you now," you respond and I smile because I'm happy you can joke about us again.

You move on top of me and I revel in feeling your weight. We kiss, exploring each other's mouths, and I taste myself. As you rub up against me, I feel myself growing hard again and I know that if you have the patience to take it slow, you'll make me come again.

You play me like an instrument and when you eventually push into me, bearing over me, my knees pulled up to give you access, I gasp. We only had sex a few hours ago, but it feels like a different lifetime and it means so much more, even though now, I know we'll do this again, many times, while earlier it felt like a final goodbye.

"Christ, you feel good," you manage to utter and all I can think of is that I want to be able to do this without condoms again soon.

"I love you," I say again, but then it bears repeating. Your movements are slow, deliberate and I think how much we've progressed since our very first time, when it was more of a sprint than a marathon. I know you're close, but you're waiting for me and I want to help myself along, but you're grinding so close I can't get my hand between our bodies. You hit all the right places, though, and I know it's just a matter of time as I get lost in your embrace and the feeling of my hands on your naked skin and your mouth covering mine. Just when I think I'm running out of breath, you speed up and I grab your buttocks, urging you on.

"Close," you warn. And then, "come."

I love it when you tell me what to do and this is no different. I want to be there with you, to show you how good you are to me and the best way to show you this is to take the plunge with you. Your movements are erratic now and until the last moment I don't know if I'll make it and then you push deep, your pelvic bones digging into my belly and your treasure trail rasping against my erection and I stumble over, coating both our bellies with my release. You follow moments later, groaning, pushing then stilling above me before you dive into my embrace. I'm only just lucid enough to squeeze you to me, enveloping you in my too-long arms, cradling your head as you slowly relax.

We lay like this for a long time, sticky, cold, until you shiver and I scramble for a sheet to drape over us. You get rid of the condom and wipe us up a little with the corner of the sheet before returning to my embrace.

"I meant it when I asked you to move back into our apartment."

I nod. "Were you serious about the marriage too?"

"Of course. If there's one thing my father's death reminded me of, it's that it can all be over in a split second. If you hadn't called me, I would have called you. We belong together."

I smile and kiss you gently. You snuggle closer and I know we're going to fall asleep like this. Nothing could make me happier.

"I'd be honoured to become your husband," I say.

You give a dopey smile as you drift off.

▲

About Zahra Owens

ZAHRA OWENS WAS born and raised in Belgium and therefore not a native English speaker. English is the only language she can imagine using for writing fiction, though. Being a typical only child, accustomed to being with adults most of the time, she sought ways to channel her wild imagination and m/m romance with a twist was perfect for that.

She has a weak spot for flawed characters and imperfect bodies, or maybe it's just her sadistic streak coming through. You be the judge.

Website: zahraowens.com

Blooming Marvellous
by Josephine Myles

"KY, YOU'RE WITH a first timer today, so make sure you behave yourself, all right?"

"Who, me?" I flash my most innocent smile.

Bert just gives me this "Yeah, right," look so I pout to see if I can get him to crack a smile. He ain't having any of it this morning, though. Reckon Mrs. Bert must have put sour milk in his tea, or summat.

"He's a respectable businessman so I don't want any of your shenanigans, all right? Just get the bloody flowers in and get the van back in one piece."

"Can't be that respectable, can he? Not if he's landed up here."

Bert sniffs but hands over the van keys and the planting plan for the roundabout.

"C'mon, what'd he do? Must have been pretty bad if he got landed with this rather than a fine. What'd he nick? Or did he smash something up?"

Bert sighs. "You know I'm not allowed. Just..." I think he's about to give me a clue then and I lean in so none of the other "volunteers" can earwig. "Look, he's one of your lot, okay? I don't want anyone giving him any shit for it, so you just keep busy and play nicely."

As we walk over to meet my mysterious, respectable partner for the day, I wonder what Bert means by calling him one of my lot. Wasn't like him to be coy about my race, so I didn't reckon it would be another black guy. Not a tagger, surely? Not that I think of myself that way—I'm a street artist, but still, it don't seem like the kind of thing a suit'd get up to in his spare time.

Then I see the fella in his crisp new T-shirt and spotless jeans, and bloody hell, does he look good. Mum'd probably call him a silver fox coz his cropped hair's heavier on the salt than the pepper, but he don't look all that old—not with the way he fills out those too-clean clothes. A few inches shorter than me, but all powerful shoulders, nice pecs and slim hips. I catch him looking at my raggedy jeans and I wonder if that's scorn on his face, but then when his gaze pans up I see these two spots of colour on his pale cheeks and he looks away, speedy-like.

Oh, yeah, now I know what Bert meant by calling him one of my lot. I grin and put a little wiggle into my walk. Not a full-on mince, you follow, but just enough to tease him, should he look back. And there he goes, looking back and then away again. I'm gonna have fun with him today.

"James, this is Ky, one of our regulars. He'll look after you. Got a bit of a gob on him, but he's all right. Ky, you remember what I said, yeah?"

"Yessir! Absolutely, sir!" I give Bert a salute and he just sighs, heading back to the greenhouse shaking his head.

Then I turn back to James, who's looking a bit nervous. I know I can come across a bit scary to white guys sometimes, what with the height and the shaved head n' all, but at least he's making an effort and holding out his hand. I think about kissing it, just to catch the look on his face, but then I take pity on him and give it a shake instead. Poor bugger probably can't figure out how he ended up here—he don't look like the criminal type at all. Up close he's even more like a businessman in his weekend gear, although he does have a nice bit of stubble and a sparkly earring in his right lobe. Cute. Maybe not all that uptight after all.

"All right, mate? James, innit? Climb on in, she's already loaded. Bert told you what we'll be doing yet, has he? It's nothing too challenging, just putting the blooms in on the Homebase roundabout. Worst bit's gonna be the state of your jeans by the time we've finished." I keep up a steady stream of chatter as I drive us out there, sneaking the odd look at James under the cover of checking the mirrors. He seems to relax a little, losing the furrow in his brow which only means he ends up looking ten times hotter. Shame he's way too old for me, but it don't hurt no one to look, like Mum always says when I catch her ogling boy bands on MTV.

I pull up onto the paved edging strip of the roundabout and kill the engine.

"Can you park here?" James asks, all worried sounding. "I don't want a parking ticket on top of this."

"Council van, innit? You can park wherever you bloody well want and nobody's gonna do nothing."

He just gives me this look which I think is meant to be intimidating, but it sends the wrong kind of shivers through me. Or the right ones, depending on which way you want to look at it.

"We can park in the car park if you really want to ferry all those flowers over in the wheelbarrow." I glance down at his Birkenstocks doubtfully. Didn't anyone tell him you needed proper footwear for this? "If you think you're up to dodging the traffic in those Jesus sandals."

James looks at the lorries circling around us and I can see him weighing it up. "Right, the sooner we get on with this, the sooner we finish." He rubs his hands together and looks almost keen. Heh. He'll learn soon enough.

I get James unloading the trays of plug plants onto the central lawn area and checking labels to make sure we've got the right colours together—you can't tell when the buds are closed, and Bert'll get in a right strop if we mess it up. Meanwhile I check over the planting plans. Who designs these things? Bloody idiot has no imagination whatsoever. I notice what colours we have to play with and an idea strikes me. I grin to myself and stuff the plan in my back pocket.

"So, you wanna prep the holes or stick the plugs in?" I ask, all innocent-like, and James only goes and blushes again. Sweet. "How about I get a hole ready and you stick it in there?" I brandish my trowel.

"Uh, okay. Sounds good."

I hand James his Council issue work gloves and he looks relieved to have something to do. "We'll plant a strip of red first, all along the top of the beds."

James nods and goes to pick up a tray while I stroll over to the first bed. The soil's all been prepped by Bert during the week so it's child's play digging into the soft loam.

James makes an impatient noise in his throat. "Can't you go a bit faster than that?"

"What's the rush? We've got all morning. May as well pace ourselves."

"It's not very efficient, having me sitting around waiting for you. Have you got a second trowel?"

I sit back on my haunches and stare up at him. "It's not like you get time off for getting the job done sooner, is it? How many hours did you end up with?"

He mutters something I don't catch, what with the rumble of traffic circling around us.

"C'mon, mate. I know you're not here out of the goodness of your heart or nothing. You fucked up and got caught, same as I did. What was it? Thieving?"

He gives me this wounded look. "No!" Then he starts looking worried again. "Is that what you're here for?"

"Nah, not my style. I'm an artist. You've probably seen some of my work around."

"In galleries? What's your name again?" He looks really confused now and I have to bend over to hide my smile.

"Ky Baptiste, but I don't sign all my pieces." I look up again and I can see him concentrating. His brow goes all furrowed and he gets this serious look in his eyes. I notice they're a kind of greeny-grey in the sunshine, which is weird coz they looked grey in the van. I like 'em better out here.

"I don't think I'm familiar with your work. Sorry."

"I'm sure you've seen some around the town. I don't get into galleries—we can't all be media tarts like Banksy, you know."

I watch understanding dawn, and with it a trace of disdain. "Oh, so you're a graffiti artist." The way he pronounces the last word totally rubs me up the wrong way.

"Yeah, I'm a bloody artist, all right? Not some little hoodie going around tagging lamp posts or whatever you're thinking." Bingo. He gets this shifty look and I know that's exactly what he had me down as. "I design my works. Cut all my own stencils. They're political, making a point about this fucked-up world we live in, all right?"

"Okay, calm down. I get your point."

I see him eyeing my trowel warily and I realise I've been waving it about as I've been speaking. I go back to digging my holes and after a minute or so he drops to his knees beside me and beds in one of the first plants.

"So, what piece aggravated the powers-that-be enough to send you here?"

I wonder if he's trying to be funny, but he looks and sounds genuine enough. Not sure I wanna confide in him just yet, though. "I'll tell you, but first you gotta say why you're here working with us grunts rather than paying the fine. 'S only fair."

He flushes again, just those little spots of colour airbrushed over his cheekbones, but they're a dead giveaway. "It wasn't given as an option. I think they wanted to make an example of me."

"Oh, yeah? Go on, what'd you do?"

All of a sudden he's absolutely bloody fascinated by the geranium in his hands. "Nothing that terrible. I was somewhat...under the influence."

"C'mon, you can tell me. Then I'll tell you about the time I was so wasted I tried to snog my Mum's boyfriend. That was seriously cringe-worthy. And painful," I add, rubbing my jaw and remembering the punch that landed there. "At least Mum kicked him out after that. He might have been hot as hell, but he was a proper arsehole."

James is staring at me and I realise I've just outed myself. Well, he must have realised, surely? I mean, I'm not wearing my Champion Cocksucker T-shirt or anything, but I ain't exactly subtle.

He gets this determined look, like he's bracing himself. "I insulted a police officer. It was an accident. Not the way I usually behave. I, uh, it was my birthday party and things had got pretty wild. I thought they were the stripper. I tried to help them off with their uniform and made some suggestions. Allegedly. They weren't best pleased."

God, we're not still playing the pronoun game, are we? "Was he worth it?" I ask. "Was he fit?"

James' eyes go all wide.

"Yeah mate, I can tell. That's why Bert stuck you with me. Reckon he must be trying to matchmake or summat, the soppy old git. 'Sides, I could tell by the way you checked me out. You might as well've hung a sign around your neck."

His eyes crinkle up at the edges and I decide I like it when he smiles.

"Fuck you," he says, but there's no anger behind it.

"That a promise?" I bend over further and stick my arse in the air. Yeah, I know I'm in the middle of a bloody roundabout on a Saturday morning, but I'm just planting stuff, right? "Fancy a bit of uphill gardening, do you?"

James shakes his head and chuckles. It's a warm sound and I want to hear it again.

"Get back to work," he orders. "Cheeky beggar."

"Aye aye, sir!"

After that things are easier between us and James chats a bit about music and bikes. Turns out he's got a thing for old motorbikes and has a garage stuffed full of them. I don't reckon he's as old as I was thinking, because he's into some of the music I like. Then again, he says he saw Nirvana play live so he can't be all that young. He don't say much about his job, which is something to do with project management and sounds dead boring, but he asks a bit about mine at the warehouse and gives a good impression of being interested. That's flattering coz most posh blokes like him wouldn't bother.

We take turns digging and planting and stop for a break at eleven, sitting up on the middle of the roundabout and watching the cars and vans circle around us. I share my bottle of Coke and sandwich because James hadn't known he'd need to bring anything. Means I'm still a bit hungry afterwards, but it's nice to know I could help him out a bit, what with him clearly having the advantage in age and money and career and all the rest of that rubbish.

"So what piece did end you up here?" James asks. "Anything I might have seen?"

"It was one of my tulips," I say.

James gives me this funny look. "Is that street slang for drugs?"

"Probably, somewhere. I'm talking about real tulips, though. I spray 'em on street corners that look like they need brightening up."

"And that's political how, exactly?"

I'm about to tell him to fuck off, because the tulips are special and I don't have to explain them to no one, but there's something about his gaze that's so bloody earnest I end up spilling my guts, even though it does make me sound like a right sap.

"It's about nature finding a way, breaking out through the tyranny of concrete and tarmac, innit? There was this one growing down my street when I was a kid. Looked dead cheerful, it did, just growing out of this tiny hole in the pavement." I smile at the memory. There wasn't much beautiful about the estate I grew up on, so you had to grab every fragment with both hands and cling on. "The chavs next door went and kicked it to pieces soon as they noticed. Bastards."

James just nods and looks thoughtful. Maybe he understands. Don't reckon there's many guys that would, but then again, he is wearing Jesus sandals.

"How come I've never seen you at the Feathers?" I ask him as I fold up the sandwich wrapper. It's the only gay pub in town so I'm surprised we haven't run into each other at some point before. I mean, maybe we did, but I'm sure I'd have remembered a bloke as fit as him. Even if I had been completely shitfaced.

"Not my scene any more," James says. "Makes me feel like an old fogey."

"Nah, you're more into strippers, aren't you?" I tease, nudging him with my elbow. "Or coppers."

James just gives this sexy grin and I go all warm inside like I've just downed a shot of tequila.

We're almost halfway through the blue stripes when I realise James has zoned out. I look up from my planting hole to find him staring at my arse.

"See something you like?" I ask, casual-like. It's fun making him blush.

"I...I was just trying to work out why you kids have to show your underwear all the time." James sets his jaw and probably thinks he's looking stern but with his pupils all huge like that it makes him look like he wants to rip my clothes off there and then. "Can't you pull your jeans up properly? It's bloody distracting, being able to see your pants."

"They're decent enough, aren't they?" I look down to check which boxers I put on this morning. Yeah, it's the purple ones with the cartoon robots on them. "These are my favourites."

"I'm not saying they're not nice pants. I just don't necessarily want to be thinking about your underwear right now, that's all."

"You'd rather think about my undies later, would you? When you're on your own somewhere." I leer at him. "Think about them hard, will you?"

"That's not what I meant!" James sounds pissed off now so I don't push it, but I've got this fizzy feeling inside from knowing he was checking me out again. I mean, I'm not gonna get my hopes up too much, because a posh white bloke like him isn't going to want anything serious with someone like me, but it's a buzz to think I might get a shag out of him before we go our separate ways.

By the time we've finished planting the four beds we're both knackered and sweating. We climb back into the van and the reek of hot, sweaty man-flesh is a right turn on. I try to think about other stuff while I drive coz I really don't want to be rock hard when we get back to the park.

Bert's waiting for us and tuts at his watch as I hand him back the keys to the truck. "You're late. I've got to get home for tea. You boys just make sure you unload the empties before you go, all right?"

The empty plant trays go back in one end of the greenhouse, but as we pass the shed on our way back out I have an idea.

"Hey, James, have you got a minute? I want to show you something in here." Bert keeps the keys "hidden" under an up-turned clay pot by the shed door. You'd think he'd be a bit more careful what with some of the reprobates he works with, but he's old school. Besides, there's only more gardening junk in there. He keeps the tools locked up safe in the park office.

It's dark inside what with the ivy growing over the window and it smells of creosote and dead spiders. And now James is crowding in after me, it smells of him. I draw in a deep lungful and feel the arousal go tingling all through me.

"What is it you wanted to show m—mph!" James crashes back against the workbench as I press close, kicking the door shut behind us. "Ky? What are you doing?"

It's a really stupid question because he must be able to tell, what with the way I'm working my hand down the front of his jeans and licking the sweat from his neck. I mean, it don't take an expert in body language to work out what I'm trying to tell him. His dick seems to have caught on, though, and as I grasp hold of it I can feel it stiffening. James makes this sound, kinda worried and kinda turned-on, and I start to work him with my hand. I can feel his pulse thundering under my tongue.

"Stop it!" He doesn't sound like he really means it so I ignore him. 'Sides, he's pretty much thrusting into my grip now and things are definitely getting slippery down there.

"You've got a great cock," I tell him, thinking flattery might help relax him. "So fat and hard. Bet it would feel amazing shoved up my arse."

James gives this startled groan and grabs hold of my arm. He's strong, so I have to stop wanking him, but it's sexy having him take a bit of control back so I don't mind too much. I just grind against him instead.

"Ky! I don't...You're just a kid."

"Bollocks. I'm twenty-four. Old enough to know what I'm doing." I illustrate the point by grazing my teeth up the side of his jaw then nibbling on his earlobe, right where that sweet little stud pierces his skin. I tug on it with my teeth. "I want to suck you off," I tell him, whispering it in his ear all low and breathy like them guys on the phone sex lines do.

I almost laugh at the noise James makes, halfway between an alarmed squeak and a whimper. I know I've got him. I mean, he wants this. His body does, anyway, even if his mind's feeding him some crap about me being too common for him. Too young. Too black. "How old are you then, Grandad?"

"I'm thirty-six! Hardly drawing my pension."

"Yeah? What's with the silver hair then?" I rub my free hand over his head and it's dead soft, not like the bristles on his jaw which have left my lips feeling all tender.

"I just went grey early. I don't see why I should have to dye it."

"Nah, you shouldn't. It's sexy." I cast about for the right word. "Distinguished."

"You think so?" He sounds a bit happier now, and kind of surprised, and he loosens the grip on my arm. Good thing too, coz I was starting to lose circulation.

"Yep. So, are your pubes going grey too?"

James just gasps, and before he can reply I drop to my knees. It takes me a bit longer than usual to get his jeans undone, what with the pins and needles making my hand go all clumsy, so he has plenty of time to stop me if he wants to.

He doesn't.

And he doesn't have grey pubes either.

But I'm not gonna waste breath telling him that because I want to taste him. I want it so bad I'm practically drooling all over him. Still, no point letting all that saliva go to waste. I slurp him down, all the way to the root and bury my nose in that thick bush. He smells of ripe male and my cock's like an iron bar in my pants. It ain't classy and it ain't subtle, but I hump against his leg like a randy dog as I suck his dick.

"Jesus! Ky! You'd better...Oh, Christ." James' voice goes all deep and growly and I feel his hand on the back of my head, gentle but firm. His hips start to move and he sets a steady pace. I just cling on to his bum with both hands and let him go for it, enjoying the firm flesh under my fingers and the hot meat ramming the back of my throat.

It don't last long for either of us. What with that delicious cock in my mouth and those grunty sounds James keeps making, before I know what's happening my bollocks are drawing up tight and I'm shooting a load in my pants. Dunno if that's what sets James off—I mean, he must be able to tell I'm coming what with the noise I make around his dick—but all of a sudden I feel him pulse in my mouth. I swallow around him while I'm twitching with my own orgasm, and it's like the pleasure bursts inside me, hot and thick and electric.

James ain't all that quiet when he's coming, I've gotta say. I mean, I think he's trying to be, but he's obviously a noisy bugger in bed. When he's all done I let his softening cock drop from my mouth and give it one last lick. He shudders and lets out this sexy groan that makes me want to start all over again. Instead I get to my feet and wonder what I'm gonna do about the mess in my pants. Shoulda thought about that first, I s'pose.

"That was…that was quite a surprise," James says, his voice all wavery sounding. "Um, I suppose I should be saying thank you."

"Nah, it's cool. I got off too," I tell him, just in case he really hadn't noticed. I don't want him thinking he's got to do something for me just to be polite. I mean, it would be nice to carry on with this some other time, but it's never gonna end up being the kind of thing I'm after, is it? Not with a respectable guy like him. He'd never want a boyfriend like me.

It's hard to tell what the expression on his face is in the dim light, but his movements are all jerky as he shoves his dick back inside his jeans and buttons up.

"Right, well, I should be going, I suppose," James says. I might not be able to see them, but I know he's got those red spots on his cheeks again. His embarrassment is suffocating both of us.

"Yeah, you can go out first if you want," I say, coz I need to clean up before I go anywhere, and I've just noticed this roll of horticultural fleece in the corner that looks like it might do the job. "I'll wait a bit, just in case someone's watching."

"Thanks." He sounds relieved. "Ky, it's been, uh, good getting to know you. I…I was—"

"Is that voices outside?" I interrupt, coz I really don't wanna hear any lame excuses about how he can't do this again. "You'd better scarper. See ya next week, yeah?"

"Oh, okay. Right. Bye then."

I tell myself that the obvious relief in his voice doesn't hurt, but I'm not sure I believe it. I've always been a crap liar.

By the time I eventually skulk out of the shed, James is long gone. I suck on my teeth but I can't even bloody well taste him no more.

⏶

I DO MY best not to think about James over the next week, but picking and packing only takes up so much brainpower so, like it or not, I keep brooding. The other blokes in the warehouse keep out of my way coz I keep snapping at them, and even Mum wants to know why I look like I lost a tenner and found a penny.

When I tell her about James—the edited version—she just tuts and gives me this long look that makes me want to squirm. She reckons I should ask him out next time I see him. "Nothing ventured, nothing gained," is what she says. I'm about to tell her I already ventured and all it gained me was a mouthful of spunk, but I reckon she don't want to know about that so I keep my trap shut.

Saturday comes around before I know it and it's my last day on my current Community Service order, which is why it comes as such a blow that James ain't there. I ask Bert, casual-like, what happened to him, but he just shrugs and hands me a petrol-powered strimmer to tidy the park hedges.

It's hard, sweaty work and I reckon those hedges don't know what's hit them, but after a few hours I feel like I've worked the frustration out my system. I'm just finishing up when I feel this itch between my shoulder blades, like someone's watching me.

I turn around and there's James, leaning against a motorbike the other side of the street. He looks sizzling hot in his leather jacket, but I can't help but notice he's holding two helmets and get this stupid rush of jealousy at the thought of some other guy clinging on to him. But then he grins and it's so warm I forget all about anything else.

"All right, mate?" I call over to him, keeping it casual.

"I'm good." He crosses the street to where I'm standing and I get this weird fluttery feeling in the pit of my stomach. "How are you, Ky?"

"Yeah, sweet."

We stand there for a long moment, gazes locked. It should be awkward, but for some reason it feels comfortable being with him, even with the butterflies in my guts.

"Have you nearly finished?" he asks me, looking all hopeful.

I check my watch. "Yep, just need to take the strimmer back to Bert."

James' cheeks flush and he looks at his feet. "Want to come for a ride?" He holds up the spare helmet and I grin.

On the way back to the bike he explains there was this crisis with the latest development he's been managing, and he had to spend the whole bloody morning in an emergency planning meeting with the town council, so had to defer finishing his community service. "I wanted to be here, though," he adds.

"Oh, yeah? Got a taste for gardening now, have you?"

"I've got a taste for gardeners," he says, his smile shy but kind of wicked.

I don't ask where we're going and he doesn't say, but I'm surprised when he heads out towards the ring road. It's magic, though, just clinging on to him while the wind whips past us, the bike throbs between our legs and James' heart hammers under my arms. When he pulls up to a stop just outside of Homebase, I understand why he's brought me here.

Our roundabout looks bloomin' marvellous.

I get down from the bike and take my helmet off. James follows.

"At the end of the meeting the mayor took me aside, saying I was the only gay man she knew, and asked if that design meant what she thought it did."

I look over at the Pride flags, vibrant under the May sun. "What d'you tell her?"

"I said it looked like a rainbow to me, but she said it was supposed to be rows of bunting to celebrate the royal wedding. She'd designed it herself and was rather put out about the whole thing."

"Bit late for Kate and Wills, though, innit? I mean, that was a whole month ago. 'Sides, the design looked all cluttered. Just rows of triangles like a kid would draw. That," I jab my finger in the direction of the roundabout, "That has dramatic impact."

James looks like he's trying to hold back a laugh, but it keeps escaping in the crinkles round his eyes and the chuckle in his voice. "She's had to convince the other councillors that it was meant to be that way, and is part of her ongoing effort to promote inclusiveness and reach out to marginalised communities."

"Nice one. Go Mayor!"

I punch the air then catch the way James is looking at me—like I'm a plate of posh nosh in some fancy restaurant. I take a chance and kiss him, right there in the Homebase car park. His chin might be stubbly but his lips are soft and plump and I smile against them.

Someone wolf-whistles and I can feel a flush racing over my skin. Good thing it's not obvious on me. I reckon James can tell, though, coz he pulls back and has this sparkle in his eyes like he's laughing inside. In a good way, though.

"Fancy going somewhere for a drink?" James asks. "Get to know each other better?"

"Thought we already knew each other pretty intimately," I say, just to see him squirm again. But then I take pity and I kiss him, trying to show him how I feel with the press of my lips.

"Yeah, I'd like that," I tell him, rubbing a finger along his jaw, absurdly pleased at how those silvery bristles look against my skin.

James grins, so I kiss him again.

▲

About Josephine Myles

ECCENTRIC ENGLISHWOMAN, ABSENT-MINDED mother, proud bisexual, shameless tea-addict, serial textile craft hobbyist, iconoclastic logophile and writer of homoerotic romance—Josephine Myles is all these things at once. She has held down more different jobs than any sane person ever should, and is fundamentally rebellious, preferring the overgrown yet enticing path rather than the wide and obvious one.

Jo once spent two years living on a slowly decaying narrow-boat, and was determined that she would one day use the experience as fodder for a novel. It may have taken a few years, but she got there in the end. She usually does. *Barging In*, her first novel, will be released by Samhain Publishing in September 2011.

Visit Jo's website for steamy free reads and regular blog posts.

Website: josephinemyles.com
Blog: josephine-myles.livejournal.com
Facebook: facebook.com/pages/Josephine-Myles/194637190559079
Goodreads: goodreads.com/author/show/3499509.Josephine_Myles
Email: josephine_myles@yahoo.co.uk

About UK MAT

UK MAT IS the acronym for the UK Meet Acquisitions Team, a group of authors and editors who seek to promote and share some of the very best of LGBTQ fiction. In 2011 they have produced two excellent and entertaining anthologies, one of flash fiction titled *British Flash* and one of short fiction titled *Tea and Crumpet*.

British Flash is available in e-book format on Smashwords and through JMS Books LLC, while *Tea and Crumpet* is available at JMS Books in both print and ebook, also through other online book retailers.

The members of UK MAT attend and support the UK Meet, now in its second year, providing a fun and rewarding environment for authors, readers and allies in the LGBTQ fiction community.

Feel free to visit the website at ukmeet.weebly.com and maybe you'll join us there some time!

UK MAT, the real people? We are Josephine Myles, Alex Beecroft, Charlie Cochrane, Clare London and JL Merrow.